the Girl who
Believed in
Fairy Tales
three short stories

Heidi Garrett

The Girl who Believed in Fairy Tales by Heidi Garrett

Half-Faerie Publishing

Copyright © 2014 by Heidi Garrett

The Girl Who Watched for Elves, The Girl Who Dreamed of Red Shoes, and The Girl Who Couldn't Sing were published for the first time in 2013 as single stories.

Find out more about Heidi Garrett at

www.heidigwrites.blogspot.com

All rights reserved.

This book is a work of fiction. Names, characters, places, brands, media and incidents are either the product of the author's imagination or are used fictitiously. Any resemblance to actual persons, living or dead, actual events or locales is purely coincidental.

All rights reserved. No part of this book may be used or reproduced in any manner whatsoever without written permission except in the case of brief quotations embodied in critical articles and reviews. Thank you for respecting the hard work of the author.

Cover Art by J.W.B.

With Significant Contributions from Jason Gurley

All rights reserved.

Editing by Vince Dickinson

ISBN: 978-0-9882068-8-5

Other Books by Heidi Garrett

Sign up for Heidi's newsletter!
http://eepurl.com/wWKUj

Daughter of Light
(A Young Adult Fantasy Trilogy)

Isolt's Enchantment, A Prequel
Half Faerie, #1
Half Mortal, #2
War & Grace, #3

Once Upon a Time Today
(A Collection of Stand-Alone Modern Fairy Tale Retellings)

Beautiful Beautiful
Dreaming of the Sea
The Tree Hugger
I Am Lily Dane

In Collaboration with Billie Limpin
(A New Adult Paranormal Romance)

Cupcakes and Kisses

Contents

Dear Reader,

The Girl Who Believed in Fairy Tales is the distilled essence of two decades of compulsive journal writing. Although every cheap, spiral bound notebook has long since been burnt, the spiritual gifts of that journey remain. These days, I live free from the burden of past experiences that used to baffle me. So much so that the critical periods of transformation are the only memories I choose to carry into my present and future. Precious ingots of inner gold, they attest to the resilience of the human spirit, and the real magic inherent in life. Because deep healing is a kind of magic.

As these three stories also attest, fairy tales played no small part in helping me navigate the deep, dark woods of my psyche. I was haunted by the loss of my mother as a young girl, and grew into a young adult completely disconnected from Self. The most overt symptom of my inner wounds was a never-ending hunger that resulted in an intermittent binge-eating disorder, which confounded me for years. If you've ever suffered from an eating disorder, you're familiar with the self-loathing and shame that accompanies the inability to carry out the most elementary function of feeding yourself well.

Numerous philosophies, theories, and proposed solutions to eating disorders abound. I've read and experimented with many of them. Most of them failed me. If it had not been for my faithful journal writing, I might have given up and accepted the fate of an ever-enlarging body and ill-health. But my honest outpourings strengthened some underlying hope within. So despite my repeated failures, I persisted.

How does this relate to fairy tales? I had no idea until I stumbled upon Bruno Bettelheim's *The Uses of Enchantment.* A discovery made quite some time after I'd already defeated a multitude of inner demons, fallen in love with my handsome prince, and found my place in the world. However, Bettelheim's work caused me to reframe my journey. His eloquent thesis on the power of fairy tales to nurture our inner lives mesmerized me from the first sentence:

If we hope to live not just from moment to moment, but in true consciousness of our existence, then our greatest need and most difficult achievement is to determine meaning in our lives.

Further study of Bettelheim's analysis engendered an epiphany within me, and so I set about telling how three of the most pivotal episodes in my own search for meaning were fed by my love of fairy tales, as if by an underground stream.

So what is the truth in the three tales that follow?

I really did spend an afternoon with a tarot reader who began my reading with this statement: The world you were born into was very hot. And my father really did give me an LP recording of Grimm's fairy tales, which included a narration of *The Elves and the Shoemaker*, when I was a child. And my introduction to the world and paintings of Frida Kahlo really did transform my way of seeing, being, and experiencing the world.

I really did listen to Clarissa Pinkola Estes's audio recording of *The Red Shoes: On Torment and The Recovery of Soul Life* more times than I can count over a seven-to eight-month period, and it really did nurture my will to create a life that truly suited me.

I really did spend 15 years pursuing my dream of becoming a singer/songwriter, despite the fact that I really couldn't sing. The point being: Not only did this stubbornness create countless incredible experiences and relationships; it really did lead me, by way of a very circuitous path, to become a writer of fairy tales. And if I'd not taken that overtly futile journey, I might not have met my husband, he might not have fallen in love with me, and I might not have ever given myself the permission to experience real joy—in my opinion, the final destination of any healing journey.

I dreamed about writing the *Once Upon a Time Today* collection for many years before I settled on writing contemporary fairy tale retellings as novellas for more mature readers. By more mature, I mean those of us who have already left home. Although we might not be children anymore, we're still navigating mysterious and treacherous terrain in this world where being who we really are is becoming more and more of a blank canvas. With the freedom many of us have to define ourselves in ways that feel authentic, I wished to create a collection of stories that presents different ways of being, having relationship, and finding meaning in this world.

As I've traveled on my individual path, I've embraced many diverse philosophies, belief systems and values: spiritually, politically, and psychologically. Continued growth has forced me to question these way stations, and oftentimes move on. The characters in each *Once Upon a Time Today* novella do so as well. No one story or character in the collection defines my beliefs or values, but like a prism, each one of them refracts unique approaches to reveal the world.

This is a collection where I play Trickster, delighting in confronting cherished beliefs and ideologies (often my own!) which are at times as damaging as they are helpful. So, although I no longer agree with all my characters actions, or the ideologies they espouse in this collection, I do appreciate the way each paradigm has contributed to my own understanding of Self, this incredible journey we call Life, and the truth that most belief systems are simply receptacles that one day must be smashed if we're to continue the forward movement in the evolution of our consciousness.

Sincerely,

Heather Baker aka Heidi Garrett

The Girl
Who Watched
for Elves

1. The Tarot Reader

1984 –

On a crisp fall day, a young woman with an exhausted heart visited a tarot reader. Although she hoped he might reveal some insight, guidance, or revelation capable of transforming her entire life, she remained skeptical and stiff as she settled in a high-backed chair. The cost of the session was more than she felt like she could afford, and yet here she was.

Although she was often accused of being dreamy, not there (Where are you? Land! Earth to Heather), she prided herself on her pragmatism. If the man proved to be a hack, it would be a blow to more than her pocketbook.

Wary of him reading verbal and non-verbal cues (she'd heard stories of fake psychics who did this), she erected a careful edifice of reserve and stillness as he shuffled the cards. However, when, the reader proffered the deck for her to cut before proceeding to lay out twenty cards in two rows of ten, her anticipation intensified.

He gazed at the tableaux, then at her, then back at the cards. He adjusted his glasses and settled one elbow on the table.

What did he see in the cards?

"The world you were born into was very hot," he said.

She kept her head down, but her eyes widened. Shot like an arrow whose aim was true, the statement hit its target: the first years of her life, as she perceived them anew.

Once upon a time, a girl was born into the heat of battle. This battle wasn't apocalyptic in the sense of the world at large, no, the battle she was born into was microscopic in relation to the billions of people on Earth and the problems that plagued them. But she was only an infant, with a newborn's limited ability to move, and no ability to leave the battlefield. So to her, it was like being born into Armageddon.

Her mother and father were determined to vanquish one another. In a future not so distant, they would both be victorious.

Until then, their daughter became a weapon—another thing to hate between them.

"If we'd never had her, we would already be divorced," the father would sneer.

"It was no immaculate conception," the mother took great pleasure in reminding him.

There was an older sister, too. She often wondered: If the new addition to their fractured family were to disappear—POOF!— would things go back to the way they'd been before the war? But the older sister was uncertain whether the arrival of the younger sister was the cause of the war, or just a critical element in the escalation of aggression. Either way, she didn't much like her either.

A lot of plates were thrown.

No one ever spoke in a calm voice.

Doors slammed.

Walls shook.

Rage simmered on the back burner.

And the girl learned not to cry, because, after all, what use was it?

Everyone just shouted over her.

"Yes," the young woman told the tarot reader, "you could say it was hot."

He looked at her expectantly, perhaps curious. Or maybe he just wanted details to confirm his occult acumen.

She hesitated, because sometimes it was hard to remember exactly what had happened. It had been a long time ago and everything was different now. Sometimes, she wondered if it had all been a bad dream, and the truth of it was that she'd erupted from her father's head at the age of five, like Athena, the Goddess of War.

But then, she noticed the tarot reader's eyes were blue, like a cool and inviting pool of water—and more memories surfaced.

After the war had been both won and lost, i.e. after the mother and father had gutted and dismembered the love that had once inspired them to exchange marriage vows in the first place, the entire family arrived in Divorce Court.

The mother and father seemed quite pleased with the emotional violence and public disgrace they'd inflicted upon one

another. That neither resembled the person they'd fallen in love with, in the least, heartened them both as they prepared for the final skirmish.

Who would possess their daughters?

Of course, it was no longer a question of love or caring, since all such fragile sentiment had been extinguished on the battlefield. It was more an opportunity to slam the sword to the hilt into the opponent's heart, and both were eager to finesse the final mortal blow into the body of what had once been their family.

In those days, Divorce Court was a different creature. Joint Custody didn't exist. Mediation was an impossibility. A fight to the death was encouraged.

To prepare, the daughters were assigned numbers because names were too complicated for court recorders, and lawyers, and judges, and the state to keep track of. Private investigators were hired assassins, elder family members were recruited like double agents. This final battle—the custody battle—was going to be one for the history books.

❦ ❦ ❦

The first card in the tarot reader's tableaux depicted a smirking man sneaking away, his arms full of swords. "Lies and deception," the reader said.

The girl's tongue itched. "It's what my family knew best—how to hide the truth. Carefully layered in lies, like butter rolled into the dough of a flaky pie crust."

The tarot reader nodded, encouraging her, as his gaze dropped to the spread configured before him. He pointed to a second card, which looked like a medieval tower exploding. Bodies flew through the air.

"Yes, it was kind of like that after my father won the custody battle." The young woman squirmed—they'd reached the part of the story she hated the most, because it brought her to the last day she saw her mother alive. She was not quite five.

2. Real Mothers, Fake Mothers

In preparation for a court-approved visit, their father and newly acquired stepmother sat the two sisters down. Under no circumstances were they to reveal to their real mother that their father had re-married, or that this other woman now lived with them. They were to hide this truth as if their lives depended on it, and if pressed for any details about their life with their father, they were to lie.

The girls were delivered to neutral territory as if it actually existed, the home of their father's parents. His mother was the reason her son had eloped in the first place.

The grandmother showed a sour face when she opened her front door to find her boy's ex-wife on the welcome mat. The unwelcome woman's daughters cowered against a plush velvet sofa. The grandmother's distaste hung heavy in the air when she relocated to the next room to eavesdrop. An uncomfortable silence of frowns and downcast eyes descended upon the reunited trio. Finally, the youngest girl took her mother's hand, pulled her out the back door and into the enclosed yard. The older girl followed.

The mother perched on a swing, somber and judged. The oldest girl twirled beneath a fig tree, disconnected, as if her mother wasn't present after many long months of absence, while the younger one caught glimpses of their grandmother's harsh gaze through the kitchen window.

In this way, the girls grew wary of the woman who'd once carried them in her womb. Bone of their bone, flesh of their flesh. She would soon become a stranger.

This would please their father, and he would reward them with ice cream and candy. Wise in the ways of "people believe what they see" or perhaps "people see what they believe", he always showed good cheer and generosity during his trips with his girls to the neighborhood ice cream parlor. If anyone who had witnessed these displays had been asked if he was a good father, their answer would have been a vigorous yes, heads bobbing like puppets on a string. Would their answer have been the same if they'd known how he whipped the younger girl—in a less public place—until she learned to never ask for her mother again? A memory that would become buried so deep in her flesh, it would take years, and the promptings of one who had witnessed the assaults, to re-surface.

Recalling those days was unpleasant for the young woman, perhaps because she'd done exactly as instructed. In every degree, the truth had been hidden, she'd cannily lied, and when she'd watched her mother drive out of her life for the last time, she'd been a big girl and hadn't cried.

The tarot reader pointed to a card. The image was dark, a corpse with ten swords speared in its back.

"Yes," she said. "It was something like that."

The tarot reader pointed to another card, which depicted a moon with a woman's face. Tears rained down from the dark night sky onto a road that led to a castle. Along the road, two wolves howled, and a scorpion climbed out from the water. The card was called The Moon.

"You were betrayed," he said. "Sacrificed." He pointed to the next card, a cartoon heart pierced with three swords. Behind the central image, dark clouds roiled and visible tear drops—identical to those drawn on The Moon—fell from a thunderous sky.

The young woman appreciated how the tears on both cards were the same. They gave the cards, and the story of her life, a continuity she often longed for.

"My father and his wife had two children. It was my job to take care of them," she said.

"It was more than that," the tarot reader held the remaining deck in his left hand as he gestured with his right.

"It's true," the young woman said. "My father needed to treat someone like garbage. Once he'd thrown my mother out with the trash, he came for me. When I was younger it confused me. He'd fought so hard to possess me; I believed I meant something to him."

"And now?" The reader asked.

"We don't talk much."

He nodded. "And what about his wife?"

"She was difficult."

The bright sun ducked in and out of moving clouds. The girl crossed the mostly empty baseball fields behind the school, on her way home. Her book pack was on her back, and she was hopeful.

By the time she reached the back door, she was excited to tell her stepmother about her day. Perhaps the good grades she'd gotten would make her father's new wife like her better. Perhaps she'd stop pulling her hair and slapping her in the face.

She put her hand on the silver knob of the back door, but before she could turn it, the door flew open.

The girl's heart sank into her toes.

Brown eyes, burning with malice, skewered her. Fingernails dug into her bare arm, and she was dragged through the home to the room she shared with her sister.

Her stepmother shoved her into the room. Everything the girl owned was piled like a mountain between two twin beds.

"Clean this up!" Her stepmother punched the back of the girl's head.

Bewildered, she tripped and knocked her temple against one of the nightstands. When she'd left for school that morning, everything had been tucked away inside drawers and closets.

Her stepmother yanked out a few more drawers and added their contents to the pile. "You must learn to fold things the right way. You must do things the way I showed you."

The unspoken words, "Not like your mother showed you," hung in the air.

The girl understood. Numbly, she reached for a t-shirt and folded it on the bed. Her fingers trembled.

Her stepmother boxed her ear. "That's still not right—look at those wrinkles!" She grabbed the t-shirt, wadded it up, and threw it in the girl's face. "Now, fold it right!"

The girl became an automaton. Machine-like, she spread the t-shirt out on the bed. This time she folded the shirt more carefully.

"Go, put it in the drawer," her stepmother commanded.

The girl marched with robot legs.

"Now, clean this mess up."

"Cruel?" the tarot reader asked.

A knot formed in the young woman's stomach. It was still hard to tell the truth, so she just nodded.

He pointed to a beautiful card lying next to the wounded heart. A woman with long blond hair stood in a river, water flowed through her fingers. A nightingale sang in a tree beside her. A bright star shined in the sky.

"But you weren't alone. There was someone, or something around you, that sustained your spirit."

The young woman's body relaxed. "Yes, the fairy tales."

The reader encouraged her to say more, as was his habit.

3. Elva and the Shoemaker

The girl's father made a lot of money. He and his wife talked about it when he wasn't working. Working meant he went away on long business trips. When he came home, he brought the girls presents. Pretty dolls, funny bags, a skirt or a shirt, maybe a pair of sandals—like girls in foreign countries wore. But the girl's favorite presents were the books. And the best day of all was when her father came home with a small record player and an album called *Grimms' Fairy Tales*.

That night, when she listened to the record for the first time, her room filled with swirls and sparkles. It was like magic, which the girl believed in, because so many unexplainable things had happened in her life.

She listened to the record as often as she could. She learned about elves and enchanted selves, and being tricked and trapped in dungeons by wicked witches who were hard as nails.

And the girl began to imagine that the kind voice of the narrator, who told the stories on the record, belonged to her real father—the one his new wife had locked up some place far far away.

And she began to think that her father was rather clever for sending a message to her from his real self.

And she decided that probably, one day, she would rescue him, because now that her real mother had disappeared, he was all that she had left.

"The stories gave me hope," the young woman said.

"Hope?"

She gave him a wistful smile. "I thought if I became stronger, then I could go to war with my stepmother and vanquish her. That my father wanted me to do that for him."

The reader pointed to the next card. A wizard lorded over seven floating cups of gold against a backdrop of clouds. Among other things, a dragon and a rainbow, an octopus and a fairy, spilled from the cups. "Castles in the air," he said.

The young woman exhaled. "I was naive. I fought with the truth. She fed him lies for dinner—he preferred their sweet taste to the bitter greens I offered."

"I'm sorry," the tarot reader said.

She tapped the card, The Seven of Cups. "Even though he was the one to bring me fairy tales, he didn't believe in Happily Ever Afters. I had to leave him to his fate. It was a hard lesson, but I learned it."

The reader pointed to the next pair of cards. On the first was a lonely figure bowed in sorrow. Nine swords hung in the air behind her.

The young woman shifted in her seat. "I'm cut off from my father and sister now. I suppose when I think about it—which I make a point not to do—it upsets me." Her eyes hurried on.

The second card showed a skeleton dressed in black armor, riding a gaunt gray horse. Bone fingers gripped the rod of a black banner. In the foreground, a supplicant pleaded for mercy.

The young woman didn't need the reader to explain. "A while back, I went in search of my mother. I didn't realize how much I needed to see her. I'd been waiting for years, with the hope of our reunion stashed away inside me, like a diamond swallowed whole. When I found out she'd died, and that I'd never have the chance to say goodbye, or tell her that I loved her, that diamond turned to coal. I choked on it. The world stopped around me, but it kept moving for everyone else. I'm still trying to catch up."

The tarot reader nodded, offering a moment of respectful silence as the remains of the young woman's grief settled between them. "Would you like something to drink? Perhaps, some hot tea?" he asked.

"Maybe some water."

He returned with a full glass.

After she took a few sips, the dark moment passed.

"Ready?" he asked.

The young woman wrapped her arms around her stomach. "Yes, let's finish this."

He indicated the tenth card, the last one on the bottom row. A tiny man with glasses hunched over a workbench, hammer in hand.

The young woman laughed, "That's an elf."

Of all the fairy tales in the Brother's Grimm collection, the girl's favorite had been *The Elves and the Shoemaker*. The story of elves who rescued a humble craftsman and his earnest wife thrilled her heart the first time she'd heard it.

Maybe it didn't matter if her good grades meant nothing to her father or stepmother. Maybe it didn't matter if they didn't notice when she tried to be kind or good. Maybe, she needed to look to another source for recognition and reward.

She decided to try harder; to pay more attention to her studies; to do her chores without being prompted; to be more patient with the children of her father's second wife.

And yet there was more to the story.

Her fake mother had taken the two younger children to a birthday party. Her older sister was studying with a friend. The girl had been left at home to do her chores. She didn't mind, the peace and quiet were soothing. And if she finished the laundry and ironed her half-sister's school uniform—if she finished dusting all the expensive figurines her father had shipped from Hong Kong—if she vacuumed the dining room and emptied the dishwasher before they got home—then she could listen to the

Brothers' Grimm for a few moments, undisturbed.

With that motivation, she attacked her chores with a wellspring of enthusiasm that was usually difficult to muster. When she finished folding the clothes, she began to put them away. But which drawer did her stepmother's nightgown belong in? If she put it in the wrong place, she would be grabbed and shaken until her teeth rattled. She stared at the chest of drawers in the home's master bedroom—it must be one of the smaller ones.

She opened the top drawer and slammed it shut—panties and bras. She opened the one beside it. That wasn't it either. She opened the one below it. No. Maybe it was the one at the bottom. She leaned over to open it. That looked right. She placed the nightgown she'd folded as best she could on top of the pajamas she saw there. As she spread the nightgown to look flat, like her stepmother had taught her, she felt something bulky below the pajamas.

Curious, she pushed her neat work aside.

A pack of papers, tied with a pale blue ribbon, hid among the soft, silky clothes.

Her eyes widened. They were addressed to HER.

27

She touched the packet. It was real. She wasn't imagining it. She ran to the front of the house and peeked out the window. Her stepmother's car was nowhere in sight. She raced back to the master bedroom. Her heart springing, she took the package from its hiding place and set it on the floor beside her feet. She smoothed her stepmother's nightgowns and slammed the drawer shut.

Forgetting the rest of her chores, she took the bundle of letters to her bedroom. She sat on her bed with her heels banging against the boxspring. The weight of the letters in her hand was substantial. She tugged at the ribbon and turned the first envelope over. The seal was broken, it had already been opened. Inside was a fragile piece of paper folded in thirds. She took it out. A spidery black script scrawled across the page. Some of the words were hard to read, but the writer of the letter wanted to know about HER, the girl.

How was her new family? What about her new home? Did she have any pets? How was she getting on in school? Did she know that her mother missed her?

The girl's heart wedged in her throat.

Her real mother missed her?

The girl's lips compressed. Her real mother's name had not been uttered in her father's home for years.

A black butterfly fluttered in her stomach, secrets and hope.

She turned the letter over. There were a few more lines. And then it was signed with a magic word: Elva.

The girl stared hard at the word, because she understood this might be the most important moment in her entire life.

Who was Elva?

The sound of a car engine roared outside her bedroom window.

She stuffed the letter back into the envelope, made a jumble of the bow, and pelted toward the master bedroom. Out of breath, she replaced the packet of letters where she'd found them and rushed to cover them with the nightgown. Stacks of folded clothes still remained on the large bed behind her. She filled her arms and ran to put them away.

When her stepmother found her, she said, "I'm glad to see you weren't being lazy while we were gone."

The girl continued her tasks. It didn't matter what her stepmother did or said anymore. The only thing that mattered was finding who'd written those letters that were stolen from her.

The next day was Thursday, the girl's favorite day of the week. Her stepmother took her two children to the ice skating rink straight from school. The boy was on an ice hockey team, and the girl was learning to figure skate. The older sister had band practice. The girl could do whatever she wanted.

She decided she was going to stop at the public library on her way home from school. One of her teachers had told her class that you could find the answer to any question in the world at the library. There was a branch between her school and the house close enough for her to walk to by herself.

The building had shiny glass walls that reflected her image as she approached the entrance. When she looked closer, she could see fluorescent lights, shelves of books, and shadowy figures inside. She began to skip. When she reached the front door, she pushed hard. It swung open so wide that she launched forward. But she didn't fall. She took that as a good sign.

There was a big desk to the right with two elderly women behind it. The girl advanced toward the counter. She stood on her tiptoes and waved. The woman with the half-glasses sliding off her nose looked up.

"Can you help me?" the girl asked.

The woman stood up to lean over the counter. "Of course, what do you need?"

"I need to find Elva."

"Is that the name of a children's book? I've never heard of it."

"No, it's the name of a person."

The woman came from behind the counter. "Then you need a telephone book." She led the girl through the tables in the middle of the library. "Do you know Elva's last name?"

"No."

The woman stopped. "We won't be able to find her in the telephone book if you don't know her last name."

The girl felt like a stone had gotten trapped in her ribcage—it banged hard against her heart.

The woman crouched down in front of her. "Do you know where she lives?"

The girl shook her head.

"No, I suppose if you did, you wouldn't have asked me for help."

The woman pushed her glasses up the bridge of her nose and

peered at the girl. Behind the lenses, her pale, milky blue eyes were large. "Can you tell me anything about her?"

"She wants to know how I'm doing. I need to tell her."

"How are you doing?" the woman asked.

The girl twisted her fingers. If she said she wasn't okay, she would get in a lot of trouble.

When her dad had first married his second wife, some nice people had come to visit her and her sister. Social workers from Divorce Court. They'd asked the girl how she was. She'd told them about the night she and her older sister had slept on the couch with their feet in each other's faces. The stepmother had given the girls' bedroom to a friend who'd come to visit while their father was on a business trip. When the girl had asked if she could sleep in her bed, her stepmother had smashed her in the mouth. The next day her lips had been puffy, and she'd been really tired at school.

She'd also told the social workers about the time her older sister had gotten sick and puked in the bathroom. Their stepmother had pushed her sister so hard against the bathroom wall that her hip had been bruised the next day. She made the two girls clean up the vomit.

A few weeks later, the stepmother had gotten a phone call. After she hung up the phone, she shook and hissed, she screamed and spit—she even frothed at the mouth—before she kicked the girl in a place that hurt really bad.

The girl finally understood. She wasn't ever, ever, ever supposed to tell anyone that she wasn't okay, ever again.

"I'm okay," she said. "I just really need to find Elva."

"It's a pretty name," the librarian said. "Let's go see if my friend can help us." She took the girl's hand and led her back to the large desk.

"Barb, do you know anyone named Elva?"

The woman's eyes twinkled. "I wish I did." She smiled at the girl. "Elva is another name for elf, and we sure could use one or two to sneak in here tonight." She pointed to a stack of books that was taller than she was.

"Do you know the story about *The Elves and the Shoemaker*?" the girl asked.

"I sure do."

"It's one of my favorites," the girl said.

The two women exchanged glances.

"Mine, too," the woman said.

33

The girl's imagination swirled. "Do you think elves ever write letters?"

"I don't see why not," the woman said.

A sense of wonder flooded the girl's heart.

Maybe the elves who'd helped the shoemaker and his wife had come at night when she was asleep. Maybe they'd tried to help her because they knew how sad she was, but her stepmother had told them to go away. Maybe, they'd slipped their letters under her pillow, and her stepmother had found them when she was at school.

Maybe they knew where her real mother was.

Maybe she needed to watch for elves.

When she got home, her stepmother's car was in the driveway.

"Where have you been?"

"At the library," the girl said.

"You waste too much time living in a dream world."

The girl didn't argue, even though she knew her stepmother was a big fat liar and a thief. That night she watched for elves.

With every creak and rustle, she sat upright in her bed, searching the darkened bedroom with a fast-beating heart.

There was not a cheery night visitor to be seen.

The fifth time she thought she heard a giggle, the girl slipped from her bed and tiptoed to the floor-length window. Kneeling, she wiggled the stiff shade to peek out onto the front lawn. Her eyes scanned the shrubbery then ascended the yard's lone tree, branch-by-branch. She started. And rubbed her eyes.

The pair of dangling feet in pointy shoes had disappeared.

Where had they gone? She struggled to open the window. Newly painted, the frame wouldn't separate from the sill no matter how hard she pushed or pulled.

"What are you doing?" Her sister remained lying in bed, propped up on her elbows.

"Nothing," the girl mumbled. She wasn't about to tell her sister about the elves. Or the letters. Her sister had grown into a first-rate tattle tale, exchanging information about her younger sister's "misdeeds" for favors from their father. "Nothing," she huffed again.

In the moonlight filtering through the gap in the shade, her older sister's eyes narrowed.

The girl crawled back in bed as the lump in her throat swelled to the size of a softball. She stared at the ceiling while she waited for her sister's even breathing to return. The girl began to drift off. Before she knew it, it was morning.

The elves were gone. She'd missed them—again.

The next time the girl had the chance to take back her letters, they were gone too. It felt like falling into a deep, dark well full of ash and bones.

What if the elves had given up on her because she'd never written them back?

The girl's hope curled in on itself and suffocated. She tried to pretend it didn't matter. She tried to tell herself she was silly for believing in elves and fairy tales. She tried to convince herself the world was an awful, rotten place.

But the smallest chip of her heart remained beating, and she never stopped watching for elves.

4. Two Lives in One

"The remaining years in my father's home passed like a dark enchantment. One long, colorless blur."

"The first ten cards show your foundation," the reader said, "but something changed. The next ten cards represent your present and your future. Look how different they are from your past."

The young woman pointed to the first card on the top row—a single bejeweled cup, overflowing with water, clouds, and doves. "What does that card mean?"

"The Ace of Cups? It's a card of blessings. Blessings received from love."

"Could The Ace of Cups be interpreted as grace?" the young woman asked.

"Yes, that would be an excellent interpretation."

The young woman laughed as her gaze pinged back and forth between the last card on the bottom row and the first card on the top row. "Watching for elves."

The reader's eyes tensed with questions.

"My grandmother's name is Elva," the young woman said. "Elva is also an Old English word meaning *elf*. Everything changed when I found her."

The yellow cab pulled up in front of a small, dilapidated home sinking into the garden surrounding it. The girl, who'd grown into a distrusting but cautiously optimistic young woman of twenty-four, watched wide-eyed as a petite figure in a white ruffled blouse and plain black skirt flew out the front door. The old woman didn't pause on the porch, nor did she stop when she reached the bottom of the steps.

By the time the young woman had exited the cab, the white-haired woman stood beside her, squinting through thick glasses. "Heather, is that you?"

The young woman could only nod.

It was the first time in more than two decades that she'd heard her name said with love. She marveled at the difference.

A stout man, wearing slippers and a five o'clock shadow, came out of the house.

"That's your Uncle James," her grandmother said. "James, help her with her bags."

She only had one.

The woman clutched Heather's arm. "Let's go inside."

Incredulous that this odd, but welcoming pair could be related to her, the young woman followed them into their home.

Sitting on their sofa, a strange thing happened to her body. The sharpest edges of her knees and elbows softened—the grit lodged between her bones for years whirled away—and the steel that made her heart a hand grenade smelted.

She'd finally made it home.

Grace.

"Your relationship with your grandmother must be very special," the reader said.

"It is."

"But it hasn't fixed everything, has it?"

She hated to admit there were still gaps in her life. "No."

The reader tapped a card. There was an image of an old man, brandishing a lantern in the dark. He walked with a staff and wore a pointed hat. "In many ways, you're still alone, searching."

"It's true. My grandmother doesn't live in this city, and I only visit her once a year."

The tarot reader nodded. He pointed to the next card. A mysterious woman, dressed in long robes, with a strange horned hat on her head, gazed from it. "Whatever you're seeking, you're going to find it."

His statement pleased the young woman. Yet, there were so many days when she lost her faith, she couldn't help but ask, "Really?"

"This is The High Priestess," he said. "The keeper of life's mysteries. You're learning to trust your instincts now, is that right?"

"I used to be so numb, it was like I didn't even have instincts," she said. "Now I get these wispy sensations. Sometimes, they're only images in my mind, other times they're swimmy feelings in my stomach. The strongest ones are the walls that slam my heart shut, No, not that way! I've learned to listen to the wall, but sometimes, the swimmy feelings and images are so ephemeral." The young woman recalled regrettable decisions she'd made when she'd ignored that guidance from within. "If I don't pay attention, they float away. But days, weeks, months later, when my life has reached some new dead end, they come back— mocking me, haunting me." The young woman shook her finger. "You didn't listen!"

"Why do you squelch your instincts?"

The girl's stomach heated. "Sometimes it just seems so hard— impossible—to go the way they're telling me to go. Or they just don't make any sense because they seem illogical."

The tarot reader picked up the The High Priestess. "Your instincts are the God Voice within. Trust them—" He picked up the next card in line. "—and you will have this." A bright sun shined down upon a laughing child who was waving a brilliant red flag and riding a snow-white horse. "The Sun."

"Really?" The young woman asked.

"It will be a breakthrough as life-changing as finding your grandmother."

The young woman's heart tingled. When her friend had recommended that she come for this tarot reading, she'd doubted. It had sounded like an awful lot of money, and for what? This wasn't her first experience with the occult. She'd been to a palm reader who was a fraud. It had made her feel like an idiot. But now...she reached for The Sun.

He gave it to her.

A bright future burst in her chest. Could you put a price on that? "Wow," was about all she could manage.

"Are you seeing anyone?" he asked.

"We broke up a few weeks ago."

"Is there any chance you'll get back together?"

"No, if I've learned anything in life, it's this: Don't go back because the reason you left will still be there. So better not to leave at all until you're certain."

The reader pushed his glasses back up his nose, thoughtful. He didn't disagree. "The next two cards, The Lovers and the King of Wands, represent energies that will be coming into your life."

The young woman leaned forward. "When?"

The reader pointed to The High Priestess. "When you learn to trust your instincts. It's the only way you'll find him." He touched the King of Wands. "And believe me, this is someone you want to find. He's creative, fiery, and passionate—a natural born leader—with a strong sense of honor."

The young woman's heart jumped. To have a man like that in love with her! She bit her tongue so she wouldn't ask, "Really?" again, but she could feel delight reach her eyes.

"You have a beautiful smile," the reader said.

Giddy, she leaned to the side, her hands holding the edge of the table. "Now, you're telling me everything I want to hear."

The reader pointed to the first ten cards, her past. "Was that true?"

She sat up straight. Her jaw tightened. The past always sobered her. "Yes."

He pointed to the top line of cards. "So is this."

The young woman let that penetrate her doubt.

"When you do trust your instincts, and you find him, The World will fall into your lap."

A woman danced in a wreath of leaves; she held a baton in each hand. The card's corners were filled with the head of a lion, a bull, an eagle, and a woman's face.

"What does that mean?" the young woman asked.

"It means the journey you began the day you were born will be complete." He pointed to the bottom row of cards again. "Those things—the war, the loss, the heat—will always be a part of who you are, but you'll experience a rebirth. It will be a completely different life. You'll live two lives in one."

"That's kind of fantastic," she said.

He pointed to the eighteenth and nineteenth positions in the twenty-card spread. She saw a woman holding a scale, and an enormous sword plunging upward into the sky. "Your truth will always be important to you. In the past, you might have had a hard time expressing, even knowing, what's true for you. With more experience, you'll become more clear and capable of sharing the things you're intensely passionate about with diplomacy and grace."

"That's kind of lovely," she said.

"It is."

"And the last card, The Magician?" she asked. "The one on top of the elf?"

He settled his chin in his hand.

She waited as he seemed to study the entire spread intently.

"In a reading," he began, "it's important to take the surrounding cards into account for an accurate interpretation. In the tarot, The Magician symbolizes the bridge between the human and the divine. You see how one of his hands points to the heavens and the other one points down to the earth? In your story, The Magician sits on top of the Eight of Pentacles, or The Elf Card, as you call it. We've established that, for you, that card represents your reunion with your grandmother."

An imp of comprehension settled on the young woman's shoulder.

She recalled the end of the rainbow that had pointed the way to the apartment in which she now lived. A loft in an apartment complex of lofts, buried beneath vines and hidden by bur oaks, it was more of a tree house than anything else.

Then there was the Cherry Lane Coffee Co. that had sprouted up the previous month, like a toadstool within hiking distance of her home. Since its arrival, the young woman had made the trek for her steaming Americano beneath the weekend carnival of hot air balloons—floating overhead like primary-colored clouds—every Sunday.

And the appearance of Clemencia—only last Wednesday—who like a good witch communicated deep truths in the vernacular of poetry, empowerment, and images of Frida Kahlo. Those truths fed the young woman's dreams. So now, when she slept, her life became more daring than anything she would ever have braved in the light of day.

Except...maybe someday...

At the head of the trail that had led the young woman to each of these things, instinct had waited.

Perhaps instinct was like magic.

The young woman picked up her elf card and The Magician—bound by a common thread of seeking beyond what might be considered real. Long after she'd stopped watching for elves, she'd never given up hope in the spell of a new day—or the enchantment of dusk.

Hope had yet to fail her.

She returned the Eight of Pentacles to its spot in the tableaux. "Watching for elves, that's what I did as a child." She repositioned The Magician on the top row. "Believing in magic, that's what I do now."

The tarot reader pushed himself back in his chair. "Watching for elves, and believing in magic, that's quite the fairy tale."

Awakened to this new way of seeing her life, the young woman grinned.

The Girl
Who Dreamed
of Red Shoes

1. Bavarian Kreme Doughnuts

1989 –

Once upon a time, there was a young woman who'd lost her way. She knew her home address, and she knew how to get there, so she wasn't lost in that respect.

At night she would dream, and in her dreams she wandered a cream-colored mansion infused with golden light. It would seem as if she was floating or flying, more like a ghost than a person. When she would have occasion to look in the mirror, she would start, because the person in the reflection looked nothing like who she felt herself to be.

And so her dreams showed her: Her spirit was disconnected from her body, hovering close by, but nonetheless disengaged from her daily reality.

And you wouldn't think this would be a problem because she

was aware of it.

It should be an easy thing to coax her spirit back into her body. But it was not.

The young woman and her spirit had been disconnected for years, so even though they were familiar to each other, they weren't really acquainted.

Besides, the girl didn't want her spirit to return to her body. She'd decided a long time ago that flesh was a dangerous place for spirit to live, so she made sure her spirit never felt welcome or comfortable inside her.

Yet, the young woman suffered from longing. The longing persisted, even though she pretended that it did not.

"How's John?" Katrina asks as we head to the state-owned parking lot, next to the state-owned building, where we work at our crappy day jobs dreaming of another life.

I've been avoiding her—and this conversation—for weeks. "We broke up." I say it loud because she's moving faster than me. Her car is farther away.

"Mutual?" She's raising her voice. It sounds like she's talking from the back of her head.

Of course, she wants to know who broke up with whom. I make a face at her—stick out my tongue and scrunch up my nose. "No. Me."

She whirls around—almost catching my snarky look. "You ended it?"

"Yes."

"I don't believe you."

Immoveable, like a ten-car pileup that's smashed into my rear fender, she's blocking the path to my car's front door. I roll my eyes and maneuver past her. She tugs on my jacket.

"What?" I ask.

"He was so fine," she says. "The car, the money. I just don't get it. What did he ever see in you?"

"Maybe I was just a good beard."

Confusion clouds her narrow eyes before the light of understanding strikes. "He's gay?"

"No, I was just making a bad joke."

"Yeah, not very funny," she says.

"Things just weren't clicking."

"Weekends in New York, a red Porsche, what's not to click?"

We live in a tourist town. I'd met John one weekend at a bar on Sixth Street, one of our city's main attractions. I'd had too much to drink, he had a pretty face, and my judgment was off. We'd started hot and heavy, but the more I'd gotten to know him, the more his one-track mind for cash and status turned me off.

Hooking up with him had been the reason I'd sobered up in the first place. The last two times I'd been with him, all I could think was: What's wrong with me, and why am I with this asshole? I figured alcohol was rotting my brain and I needed to regroup. I'd come across an AA pamphlet in the airport and was pretty certain that God was speaking to me. I'd gone to a meeting —one meeting.

It was weird, but I've been sober almost two months—another topic I don't wish to discuss with Katrina. "John isn't my type," I say.

She hikes up the handle of her knockoff Chanel purse. "Yeah, what's your type—the wannabe losers in this town?"

"I'll let you know when I find out."

She snorts. "I won't hold my breath." And spins on her heels.

The Wicked Witch of the South. Maybe I'll get lucky and someone will drop a house on her tonight.

Climbing into my fuel efficient vehicle, I feel like I've survived an assault. Too bad Katrina isn't the worst of my problems. On top of another crappy day at the office, it's been another crappy day on my diet. Another thing I've discovered I'm not good at doing–dieting. Ever since I stopped drinking, all I've wanted to do is eat–correction–gorge myself.

I tap the steering wheel of my car. I'd known the diet hadn't stood a chance when I'd agreed to go to lunch at Jalisco's. The downward spiral began with the first basket of crispy tortilla chips. The only thing that had put a stop to my constant hand-diving was the fact that the waiter stopped bringing refills. And really, five pralines on the way out the door? What had possessed me?

Although the chicken breast thawing in my refrigerator sounds wretched, the thought of not eating doesn't cross my radar. Because even though I'm not physically hungry, somehow I'm starving.

I turn the key in the ignition but don't press the gas, because I haven't made up my mind. Will I walk around the lake or stop by the new, sleek, jumbo grocery? Maybe Dunkin' Donuts? I check my watch.

It's fall and already getting dark outside.

Scratch the walk. A little spring unlocks the tension accumulated from trying to control my savage hunger all afternoon. Tonight, I'm going to give it full reign, and I'm going to enjoy it.

I'll be perfect, and start my diet again tomorrow.

So what's it going to be? The Dunkin' Donuts, Pepperidge Farm chocolate chunk cookies, and a half-pound bag of M&Ms Triple Header? Or the Stouffer's frozen macaroni and cheese, chased down by Häagan-Daaz coffee ice cream, and a large bag of Mini Reese's Peanut Butter Cups Threesome?

I do everything in threes. A little obsessive, but the ritual is more important than the food—which will be tasteless. Yes, tasteless. After the first few bites, those overstimulated taste buds just shut down.

I know this, but still I'll devour it all! A good little girl cleaning her plate. Binging blunts the wretched hunger for things I don't know I want, or things I think I can't have, or things I don't know how to get. It helps me cope with a life that feels...chained.

As I back out of my parking space, I try not to think of the doctor my HMO sent me to last month. As soon as I'd quite drinking, depression had shot up like a rubber tree in the Amazon jungle. The doctor prescribed the Peace Corps.

Are you kidding? I already have a government job that I hate. I don't need a nonpaying one. The next doctor offered me antidepressants. No, thank you, to that too. Keep your synthetic meds—they might destroy my liver.

I prefer to go down in a blaze of caffeinated, trans-fat, sugar glory.

As I circle down to the garage exit, I consider the past few weeks. My binging has escalated and my depression has gotten worse. Sometimes I don't want to get out of bed. A more intelligent person might have started drinking again, but I'm determined to see this sobriety thing through. Some part of me believes that if I can just stay sober, I'm going to discover something, and it's going to be really life-changing and earth-shattering.

That thought gives me a little lift as my body swings into overdrive. It's already tweaking with the anticipation of more sugar.

I pull into Dunkin' Donuts' empty parking lot. The realization that I can't wait 45 minutes for frozen macaroni and cheese to cook has made my decision easier. I hesitate, briefly. If they don't have six chocolate Bavarian Kreme doughnuts, it's going to be a bad night. My binges are ritualistic. Each one must be repeated to perfection. I take a deep breath and pull on the handle of the shop's swinging glass door. I'm scanning the doughnut bins as if my life depended on it, because tonight it feels like it does. I sidle up to the counter. Apparently the demand for doughnuts at 5:45 p.m. on a Wednesday isn't high, so it's only me and the girl behind the counter in the store. There are seven chocolate Bavarian Kreme doughnuts in the tray. I exhale a sigh of relief.

"Can I help you?"

"Six Bavarian Kreme doughnuts."

"Sure you don't want a dozen?"

God, no. The ritual requires I finish every ounce of food I buy. If I were to take home a dozen doughnuts, I'd have to eat them all and probably explode. No, thank you. "Just six."

The girl has stains on her apron. Her bleached hair is kind of ratty. Dark eyeliner rings her eyes and there's about twenty rings on her ten fingers. She's got a tattoo on the inside of her wrist. I'd never get a tattoo, yet envy sparks. She's slim, which is the only thing I really want to be tonight.

It's not that I'm obese, I'm just kind of fluffy, and I hate it. Still, I don't know how to not come here and buy half-a-dozen doughnuts, so I can mindlessly inhale them when I get home. I don't know how to not be hungry, even when my body is already full.

So when she rings me up, I look into her eyes and smile when I hand her my money. She has something I want, and I just don't know how to get it. Yet.

2. Group Think

The young woman's eyes were closed windows, behind which her drifting spirit dozed in lightless rooms. On occasion, she would crack the blinds, and her drifting spirit would blink at the sight of something that had meaning to her.

Most often, it was something imperfect but alive–messy but vital–luminous in its defiance of everything she'd been taught was right. Yet, she was caught–standing frozen–like a girl in a row boat at the edge of a lake. With one foot on the dock, one foot on the keel, and as the boat drifted, she was at risk of falling, headfirst, into the murky waters–a baptism she resisted.

So, she kept the windows of her eyes squeezed shut and the front door of her heart bolted. She was unaware that if she lingered at the sill, or cracked the door, a path might reveal itself, a way by which she might shed her luxurious but imprisoning psychic home, free her spirit, and enter into the woods.

Because in truth, that enormous and empty shell that she called home was all she had. If she left it, she would become like nothing—a dust mote flung by the gentlest breeze into someone's nose. Gesundheit!

Or some such horrible fate.

She couldn't bear the thought.

She refused all impulses toward freedom and silenced all inner intimations, honoring the solemn vow she'd made long ago to ignore her inner cries.

That voice was as dangerous as her flesh.

It only got her into trouble.

I slam the snooze on my alarm, roll over, and cover my head with a blanket. The enchanted sleep of my sugar overdose has worn off and it feels like I've swallowed a whale. I'm so fed up, disgusted, and repulsed by myself. It's time for drastic measures, but my imagination of possible solutions is limited, asphyxiated. I'm obsessed with diets, restriction, and perfection. I have zero ability to connect my endless hunger to my daily faith in deprivation. I have nothing else to believe in.

Before I leave for the office, I shuffle through the stack of papers on my dining room table. Buried under junk mail and insurance forms is the list of meetings for people who eat too much. The idea of such a group is too revolting, shaming, and degrading to even consider. But this morning, desperation shoves me past any and all resistance.

I spend the rest of the day on autopilot.

I eat pretty much whatever is put in front of me or offered.

I don't binge or diet, but I'm completely disconnected.

After work, I pull out the list I crammed into my purse. It's wrinkled, so I flatten it on the car seat next to me. I check the meeting place, address, and time. I can make it if I leave now and don't make any stops along the way.

I drive through the five o'clock traffic, covertly observing drivers in the lanes beside me. I imagine they're all going home to perfect families, lovers, lives. No one else is feeling cut off or isolated. I don't realize my simplistic projections are just another way I torment myself.

The meeting is in a church. Having abandoned my childhood faith over a decade ago, I try not to dwell on this inconvenient fact. I sit in my car and watch other people of various shapes and sizes cross the parking lot. When it's five minutes past the hour and everyone else is inside, I take a deep breath, climb out of my car, and follow the path the others have already taken.

Inside, the meeting has already started.

I flinch. Rote recitation dominates the opening format. Stranger prayers, odd creeds, group chanting. I look at the cracks in the puke-pale blue walls, the craters in the dingy sofas, and the sterility of the folding tables forming a large square in the room's center. Finally, people start speaking off the cuff—sort of. They uniformly profess a thrill that they've arrived here in this dingy arena.

Something within me rebels. They're all grateful, but inside I'm barren. I've arrived at the equivalent of social Siberia. They ask if anyone is attending their first meeting tonight. I sink as low as possible in my seat and refuse to raise my hand although half the room stares at me expectantly. People who are willing to sponsor stand up. I'm seriously getting the creeps. I'm not going to call someone every day and tell them what I'm going to eat. Apparently, there are some lines even I won't cross.

By the time the meeting is over, I'm clear: This isn't my

solution.

But I don't binge on my way home.

3. Sustenance

That night the young woman dreamed of wastelands.

She wandered the scorched landscape in awe. Her mansion was obliterated and gray skies promised nothing but hail storms. Yet, whatever had caused such a leveling had sparked unrepentant ecstasy within her.

Far away, a line of trees—the forbidden forest—promised chthonic shelter. She marveled at her lack of sorrow, fear, and trepidation; it was the first night in a long, long time, she was not of two parts.

The atom of her psyche had split, and a neutron—something key—had been released.

The next morning, I feed the meeting schedule for people who eat too much into the shredder. As I pat myself on the back for evading the horrors of group think, I'm aware of being in a new place, trapped in some new vacuum, thrown back on my own resources.

I don't bother with breakfast. Newsflash: I'm not hungry.

At the office, I push things around on my desk. There's got to be some routine task requiring little brain power that I can attend to—something I can crank out while simultaneously hanging on to this timid sense of *joy*.

I settle on a wrinkled brown bag full of adding machine tape and smirk. Honest-to-gosh inventory records—they need to be verified. This should do the trick. Crunching numbers allows my imagination to roam unimpeded. Although I'm still eager for five o'clock to arrive, by the end of the day, I'm chatting with coworkers, smiling, and laughing.

I had a sandwich for lunch, and I'm not really thinking about dinner. I'm thinking about the new three-level bookstore I want to stop by on the way home. I used to hang out at bookstores. Just walk the aisles, pulling out an interesting title here or a fascinating cover there. Sometimes I'd come home with too many buys. Other times I'd leave with no purchases at all. But I've always enjoyed the quiet and mental stimulation that bookstores offer.

This new store is brightly lit. The directory near the front entrance breaks down what's on each of the three floors. After studying it for a few minutes, I advance to the stairs in the store's center. There are elevators against the far wall, but after sitting all day, I want to move my body. As I climb each step of the open stairwell, I crane my head. It's a beautiful store, a shrine to the written word. When I reach the top floor, I wander the aisles. I'm not looking for anything in particular.

The top floor is mostly reference books, text books, study aids, learning foreign languages, travel books. I return to the stairs and exit on the second floor. This is my floor. Half of it is covered in psychology, religion, spirituality, the occult. The other half is music and audiobooks. Again I tread the aisles with reverence, stopping to examine a tome here, a volume there. I push past the stile into the CD area. More meandering. I feel drawn to a kiosk of audiobooks. I pick up almost every single CD before my fingers settle on a black cover emblazoned with the white image of a dancer. The title in bold red letters reads *The Red Shoes: On Torment and The Recovery of Soul Life* by

Clarissa Pinkola Estes.

Something pops inside me. I look around at the other shoppers; no one is paying me any attention. I finish rifling through the kiosk, but some part of me knows: this audiobook is the thing I came here to get. I pay at the second floor register and jam the CD in my purse. I fly down the stairs and cross to the health food store on the opposite corner of the parking lot. I head to the salad bar and load up a plastic container.

I race home.

Once inside my tiny excuse for an apartment, I slide the salad into the fridge and change out of my skirt and heels. Sitting on my sofa, I turn my new CD over and over in my hands. Finally, I remove the shrink wrap and gouge at the small, annoying security tag. Slipping the CD into the player, I position my headphones, press play, and lie down with my back on the floor—staring at the ceiling.

An overture plays, and the storyteller begins her tale.

4. The Red Shoes

The voice of the cantadora, the keeper of old stories, saturated the young woman's senses. It transported her to an ancient wood, the threshold between the world of souls and the world of dreams, where she came upon a wraith, dancing in the woods. Mesmerized by the spirit's frenzied spins and twirls, the young woman settled in the roots of a gnarled tree to watch and listen. For this was her spirit, and she'd come to retrieve it.

There was a young girl, an orphan named Anna, who lived in the forest. She scraped out a meager existence, living on nuts, berries, mushrooms, and whatever vegetation she could find. Lonely as she often was, there was also a happiness in her heart. She loved to come across squirrels scurrying with nuts in their paws, or chipmunks playing hide and seek in the dirt and brush. She loved to rest in the cradle of low-lying branches and watch for blue jays. The most magical days she might catch a glimpse of a robin's red breast, because red was her favorite color.

Anna drank from rivers and streams, and sometimes if she hid in the long grass, and didn't move at all, she might see a doe bring its fawn to drink. On rare occasions, the antlered buck might join them, regal and proud.

At night, Anna searched for grassy meadows, so she might sleep beneath the stars, and when the days got shorter and colder, she searched for large rocks to provide shelter against the biting wind.

Every day she wore the same tattered dress, but sometimes she came across a swatch of dirty but colorful cloth dropped by a sparrow or a mouse. The girl collected these strips. When her pockets were stuffed with them, she went about dying them with raspberry juice so they would be red, like the breast of her favorite bird.

She began to collect string, and one day she came across a needle in an abandoned nest. Within a few days, Anna had created a pair of red shoes, funny little slippers that kept her toes from freezing, and softened the pinch of pebbles. Anna came to cherish them more than anything, because she'd made them.

One morning, she was walking along a trail in a field that had been flattened by the wheels of carriages, and that day, one of them came upon her before she had a chance to hide. A gravelly voice ordered the coachman to stop. He did as commanded. A wrinkled face, framed by gray hair swept into a tight bun, peered from the carriage window.

"Little girl, what are you doing wandering out here alone?"

Earlier, Anna had been picking fringed gentian and goldenrods, so she gripped a tiny bouquet. "Picking flowers."

"But where is your home? It's not safe for a young girl to be out here alone. Tell me where you live, and I'll take you home. Your mother and father must be worried sick about you."

"But this is my home."

The woman flung a bony arm from the carriage. Gold bracelets jangled on her wrists. "You can't live here in the wild. You must let me take you home. I'll adopt you, and send you to school, and take you with me to church on Sundays, so you might have a proper life."

Anna cocked her head. No one with such a fancy carriage had

ever noticed her before. The black sides of the carriage shined, and its knobs, and the spokes of its wheels, glittered like gold. The horses that pulled the carriage were the color of midnight, and blankets with silver tassels covered their backs. Wide-eyed, she considered the woman's offer.

"We don't have all day." The old woman ordered the coachman to open the door.

Anna took one step toward her new life.

The coachman reached for her hand. His were covered in the softest leather.

When Anna stood on the top step and was about to enter, the woman pointed to her bouquet. "Don't bring those weeds in here."

The coachman reached out his gloved hand. When he tossed the bruised flowers into the field, Anna felt a faint pinch in her heart that was easy to ignore. The woman patted the velvet seat beside her, and Anna settled next to her. When the coachman closed the door, it was hard for the girl to breath. A strong, sickly-sweet perfume came from the woman, who pulled Anna close to her rail thin body that was about as comforting as a bone.

When the carriage stopped, the coachman came to open the door. He helped Anna and the old woman down the carriage steps. The girl tilted her head back to see the roof of the house before her. She'd never seen such a building with walls of brick and eyes of glass windows. The woman gripped the girl's hand and led her inside.

There were rugs and chairs and sofas. Anna spied two birds and ran toward them, but they were made of glass and couldn't fly away. Not much fun to play with. The house smelled of must and most of the curtains were drawn, shutting out the sunlight. The woman called her housekeeper and ordered the girl be bathed.

The tub was big, and the water was so hot that it turned Anna's skin pink. The soap chafed her arms and legs, but the housekeeper pronounced her clean. There had been a commotion at the door and packages were delivered. When it came time for Anna to get dressed, she was presented with undergarments and stockings that were whiter than the clouds, a dress that was as stiff as the grass that died at the end of summer, and black shoes that were so shiny, she could see her face in them. When her long dark hair had been brushed and tied back with a light blue ribbon, the old woman pronounced that she was as lovely as a doll.

"Where are my clothes and my shoes?" Anna asked, for her tattered, handmade, raspberry-red shoes were her most treasured possession.

"We've burned those rags in the fire."

Anna gulped, swallowing the lump of sadness that welled in her throat.

On Sunday, the old woman took Anna to church.

"Pay attention. Your confirmation ceremony will be soon, and you must say and do all the right things, in all the right ways, and with the right demeanor. If you make a mistake, my neighbors will gossip and laugh behind my back. I can't abide that. Your performance must be impeccable, beyond reproach. Do you understand?"

Anna nodded although she didn't.

"We'll have to buy you a new dress and a new pair of shoes for the ceremony."

Anna gazed at the dress she wore. Maybe the fabric of her new dress wouldn't itch, and maybe the leather of her new shoes would be softer, better for running.

As the old woman and the girl left the church, Anna paused on the church's steps. A cool breeze touched her face, and she caught a whiff of pine. Her heart longed for the forest, even though the old woman insisted the woods were a wild and dangerous place.

The coachman hurried Anna along and into the coach. The old woman needed her nap.

The next day, they went to the dressmaker, who poked and prodded the girl. She pinched her with straight pins and squeezed her arms and stomach with measuring tape. Anna was glad to leave.

They stopped at the shoemaker's next.

While the old woman ordered the man about, Anna studied row after row of shoes. When she came across a pair of bright red ones, hidden in the shadows of the farthest corner of the shop, her heart leapt. She picked one up. They were made of leather as supple as a rabbit's floppy ear.

When the shoemaker found her, Anna asked, "Please, may I

have these?"

The man showed them to the old woman whose sight was failing with each passing day. The old woman turned one of the shoes in her hands. "Yes, these feel of good quality." But the old woman couldn't see their bright red color.

It felt like a hive of bees buzzed in Anna's chest as the shoemaker wrapped the red shoes up in brown paper and tied the package with string.

It was getting late.

The young woman turned off the stereo and removed her headphones. She would finish listening to the CD tomorrow. But for now, she sat in the dark. Her mind wandered. The beautiful mansion in her dreams made her think of the old woman's home —a gilded prison.

As the young woman washed her face and brushed her teeth, she thought about the dark woods. When she was done with her nighttime routine, she stared closely into the mirror. There was a light in her eyes, one that hadn't been there that morning.

The story about the loss of the girl's handmade shoes had

stirred something deep within her. As she climbed into bed, she couldn't stop thinking about them. She drifted off, into a dream.

The young woman wandered the city streets, searching. She passed by shop after shop. When she stood outside a confectionery, she pressed her face, cradled by her hands, up against the glass.

Inside, everything was red.

A funny little man, about half as tall as she was, opened the door. "Come in."

She thanked him and crossed the threshold.

There were red lollipops and jawbreakers, cinnamon flavored jelly beans and red-hots, all in the shape of shoes and boots. But the most magnificent creations were in the bakery case: Red velvet cupcakes baked in the shape of ballet slippers, and cookies swirled with cherry icing in the shape of tap shoes.

The young woman could almost hear their heels and toes click against the shop's stark white marble floor. Just looking at them made her want to leap and spring and twirl in the air.

"See anything you like?" the funny little man peered around the counter.

She pointed to the cherry-iced tap shoes. "A dozen of those."

A sly grin appeared on the man's face as he filled a bag.

"How much?" the young woman asked.

"No charge now, you'll pay later," he said.

Something quirked the young woman's conscience, but she ignored it. "Fantastic," she said.

Before she'd left the shop, she'd already eaten an entire shoe.

The next morning, the young woman rummaged through her pantry for a tin of green tea. She brewed it and then poured it into a travel-mug to take with her to the office. When Katrina asked her to lunch, the young woman asked if they could go someplace within walking distance.

On the way, they passed a garden of red chrysanthemums. The young woman pulled out a pocket notebook and sketched one of the flowers quickly while Katrina studied the French tips of her fingernails.

At the end of the day, the young woman rushed home to hear

the rest of her story.

5. The Executioner

The next Sunday, Anna put on her new dress. Although it was as stiff as the others, she was intent on her shoes and hardly noticed. The soft red leather caressed her ankles as she pulled on the laces. A spark of life stirred her heart.

When she reached the bottom of the stairs, the old woman pronounced her perfect.

At church, Anna held her head high. She advanced to the altar when it was time for her to be confirmed. The nave filled with whispers, the sound of water roaring over rocks right after the rain. Outside the church, Anna smiled at the old woman's friends. In return they gave her ugly frowns and fierce grimaces. They whispered in the old woman's ear.

"Take those heathen shoes off your feet," the woman yelled at Anna when they got home. "Give them to me—you'll never wear them again!"

The girl obeyed, but something inside her wilted. Her head dropped and her shoulders sagged as she placed her little red shoes in the old woman's claws.

That night, the woman came down with a chill. She hacked and wheezed and stayed in her bed. Each day, she claimed a new ailment. Her head was on fire, her rheumatism stiffened her bones, and her stomach refused all food. Anna tiptoed through the house. She found the closet where the old woman had hidden the red shoes. She dragged a stool to the closet but still couldn't reach the shoes. She stacked a wooden box on top of the stool, stretched her fingers, and inched the shoes down from the shelf.

Anna clutched them to her chest and ran to her bedroom.

The next Sunday, even though the old woman was too sick to attend church, she demanded Anna go. "You're—much—too—wild." The woman coughed between each word. "You must be tamed. Off to church, the coachman will take you."

Anna nodded and backed out of the old woman's room, which smelled even worse than the rest of the house. She raced down the hall. When she returned the red shoes to her feet, she couldn't help but admire them in the looking glass in the hall.

The coachman didn't notice her shoes. If they didn't hurry, they'd be late.

When Anna arrived at the church, a funny little man, dressed like a soldier, stood by the door. He was lame, his right leg injured in a war. As Anna walked by him, he said, "What pretty red shoes."

That morning, the old woman's neighbors cackled like magpies when Anna advanced down the aisle between the pews in those red shoes again. When the service was over, the same little man guarded the church exit. This time, he pointed at Anna's feet, and said, "Those look like dancing shoes."

Anna's feet twitched and her toes tapped. Her heels clicked together, and she waltzed down the church stairs. The mouths of the old woman's friends gaped. The coachman chased after her. By the time he caught her, he was panting, and his brow dripped with sweat. He had to sit on Anna to hold her still. He yanked each shoe with all his might to get them off her feet.

"Don't wear these again," he told her.

Anna gave a forlorn nod of her head.

The old woman became more ill. Every day her neighbors and friends came to the house, shaking their heads and saying their prayers. No one paid attention to Anna. One night she couldn't sleep. It seemed like the red shoes called her name. She tiptoed through the house, past the old woman's bedroom and the sleeping housekeeper. A door to a room at the end of the long hall stood ajar. Anna was certain the voice that beckoned came from within.

She entered the room. Moonlight poured through a half-open curtain. The room was empty except for a rug and a large cabinet, pushed against the wall. Anna went to the cabinet. It squeaked when she opened the door. There were five drawers inside. Anna pulled each one open. The coachman had hidden her red shoes in the bottom one. Still in her nightgown, her long brown hair trailing down her back, Anna sat on the rug and laced up her shoes.

Again her feet twitched and her ankles popped. Her body unfolded as if she were a puppet and somebody were pulling her strings. Her arms flung out, her left foot kicked high in the air.

She performed a magnificent pirouette before lunging out of the room and gamboling down the stairs.

A cold, strong wind blew the front door open. Anna did a reel all the way down the steps and into the street. When she reached the edge of the town, she lurched into a polka. Her body twisted and dipped and spun in the freezing air. By dawn, she'd reached the depths of the forest, and no matter how hard she tried to turn back toward the town, the red shoes pattered on, in a quadrille, and then a minuet. Anna danced and danced. For nights and days, her body jerked and lilted. She could do nothing to stop her frenzied elbows or knees.

The old woman died and still Anna danced on.

She danced until she became a wraith. When the old woman's neighbors and friends spied her from their locked windows, they would cluck like hens and sigh like the wind. "There is the devil's daughter. Old Gerta did her such a kindness in taking her in, and now she mocks her adopted mother's generosity and care with shameless dancing–tossing her body to and fro with such abandon. We told Gerta no good could come of a daughter who wears red shoes."

And the girl danced on and on until one night she reached the cemetery. She managed to wrap her arms around a monument, but the shoes still wouldn't stop. Her legs waved madly in the air as her arms became bruised and weak.

There, the executioner found her and offered to cut off her feet. "It's the only way you'll get those red shoes off."

With tears in her eyes, Anna gave her consent.

If her life had been hard before as an orphan, it was brutal now as a cripple.

The young woman's heart broke for Anna. She listened with full attention as the cantadora expounded. The problem was not the girl's longing for red shoes. The problem was living a life that was not hers, one disconnected from her spirit. It seemed the most important pronouncement the young woman had ever heard.

The cantadora spoke of artisans who, with intricate chips of glass created rose windows for ancient cathedrals. Her rich voice told how those windows took a lifetime to craft. Faith and dedication had been the daily sustenance of the artisans and their families until the final magnificent creation could be revealed.

The cantadora's tale of patience and time, of inner truth and savoring—her story of the handmade life—became like a thread that stitched the young woman's spirit to her toes.

So that night, when the young woman fell asleep on her living room floor, she dreamed of living at the edge of the woods. From there, she spied a beautiful mansion, but it didn't call her. She turned her back on it as she walked deeper into the forest with her spirit sewn to her ankles like a shadow.

6. High Tops

I wake up on my living room floor with a crick in my neck. Otherwise, I'm fine. Although I do check my feet, just in case.

It's Saturday, and more than anything, I want a pair of red shoes.

I drive to the mall. Even though it's early, hundreds of cars fan out from the building's odd spokes where the main entrances are located. As I make my way across the pavement, I'm struck by the turquoise sky, the coolness of the air, and my upbeat mood. I'm not convinced a pair of red shoes will change my life—or make me stop binging—but this morning it feels like I'm heading in the right direction for the first time in a long time.

For the first time in my life?

Can a child be born with its spirit unattached?

Inside, shoe stores are the only thing on my radar. I try on every single red pump in the mall. Patent leather, suede leather, satin—none of them are right. Next up: sandals. I won't say no to anything red. This means the strappy ones with rhinestones, the chunky ones with feathers, and the funky ones with neon stripes. Not one of them scream, Me!

Maybe a pair of boots. I totter around a shoe department in a pair of thigh highs, then a pair that reach my knees, and finally, a pair of ankle booties, but I still haven't struck red gold. What about slippers?

The first pair are large and fuzzy, like cotton candy, another pair fit like knee-socks.

None of them are right.

My adamant refusal to buy the wrong pair of red shoes must be a good thing if frustrating.

I leave the mall empty handed, disappointed, and hungry.

By the time I reach my car, I realize I haven't eaten all day. Searching for red shoes has distracted me from my compulsive nemesis—binging. Is the cure as simple as acknowledging that I really want something, and then refusing to give up—or settle—until I find it?

What other needs, hungers, or desires might be locked away

inside me?

Something to ponder the next time the binge beast snarls my name.

Before I drive off, I check my phone. There's a text from Raven, my goth friend, the one I really like and secretly want to be like. I call her back. We agree to go out for dinner. I head over to her place, wistful.

When I arrive, Raven isn't near ready. I don't mind. Watching her paint on her rebel face, tie her hair in knots, and rip her tights always makes the voiceless part of me giddy. Maybe I don't really want to be her—all dressed in spiky black—but I want to be me as much as she is herself. I follow her into her bedroom—a pile of color is stacked on the only chair.

"Do you mind if I move these?" I ask.

"No, throw them anywhere. Mom still doesn't get my commitment to black." She stabs her mascara wand in and out of its tube. "I've tried to tell her how powerful and freeing monochrome is, but she still insists on sending me color. It's all going to the secondhand store tomorrow."

I pick up the clothes and freeze.

A pair of bright red tennis shoes remain on the chair. "Are you taking these to the consignment store, too?" I whisper—excitement makes my voice raspy.

"God, yes," Raven huffs.

I set the rest of the clothes carefully on the bed before picking up one of the amazing and marvelous red tennis shoes. Fireworks explode in my chest. Raven and I wear the same size. "Can I have them?"

Raven stops teasing her hair. "You're kidding?"

I shake my head. "I've been at the mall all day looking for a pair of shoes just like these."

Raven groans. "You're so weird."

"Can I have them?"

"Sure, my mother will be thrilled that somebody wants them."

My mother died years ago. "I'll write her a thank you note."

Raven rolls her eyes. "Whatever."

The next day felt like Christmas. The young woman put on the red shoes. She walked through her apartment. She kicked into the air. Again and again. She twirled and jabbed her fists.

Wearing the shoes made it easier to hear her spirit whisper in her ear.

There was a park that bordered the woods a few blocks from her apartment. She crawled into the back of her closet and dug out her camera. For almost the entire day, she explored the fields and the changing colors of the trees and the sunlight—shifting from morning's pale blue to noon's golden rays and then dusk's pinkish-gray gloaming.

She snapped hundreds of pictures.

That week, every night she came home from the office, slipped on her red tennis shoes, and studied the digital images on her computer. Her fingers stretched with the desire to hold a charcoal pencil. Before long, her drawings covered the living and bedroom walls.

When Raven stopped by, she walked through the young woman's apartment, tugging on the skull that hung from her favorite spiked dog color. "Damn, you have talent," she said.

With that pronouncement, a strange, but wonderful, sensation accompanied the young woman's breathing.

She returned to her closet for the boxes of acrylics and oils, brushes and gessoes. There were a few blank canvases shoved in the back, too.

Sometimes she listened to music when she painted, but most of the time she listened to the cantadora tell the story of the red shoes and the handmade life.

The young woman thought about the relationship she'd had with the ambitious stock broker and his fiery red Porsche—the one that had inspired her to shove her paints and her canvases—her talent—into the closet of her bedroom, because they'd never make it to a gallery in Manhattan.

The relationship where she'd felt like she was starving the entire time.

That relationship had been like the dangerous red shoes—the ones the executioner had cut off Anna's feet.

But the hand-me-down red tennis shoes, like her art, were an expression of the young woman's spirit—and beginning of her handmade life.

Whenever I go dancing, I wear my red tennis shoes.

They feel like magic, setting my feet on fire. Whenever I wear them, I become fearless.

I pound their rubber soles against the floor, wave my arms in the air, and whip my head until my hair becomes a cyclone. I feel wild and free, sane and whole—all at the same time.

Tonight, they're playing 80's music. Raven and I aren't leaving anything on the dance floor. We shake and jiggle our bodies as though the club's ceiling will open like a space hatch and drop the secrets of the universe at our feet.

When Maniac comes on, we ratchet things up to hyper-drive. My t-shirt is drenched; perspiration tickles the backs of my knees. Through the strobe lights and white haze of the fog machine—

I see him.

Everything slows down.

My heart pumps a dull, ear shattering thud in my chest.

He's wearing red tennis shoes.

High tops.

With the reunion of her spirit, the young woman's handmade journey began.

The Girl Who Couldn't Sing

1. No Smiling Allowed

1993 –

Once upon a time there was a woman who didn't smile. She lived with a stern frown etched upon her face. On occasion, fleeting delight would catch her–like a doe in the headlights. Her lips would curve upwards, or she'd find herself unable to stifle a laugh, and someone would inevitably pronounce, You have a beautiful smile.

She would pass the palm of her hand over her face, erasing all signs of glee, and grimace for the rest of the day in devoted penance, because life was a vale of tears and suffering, especially for women. That's what her Bible said, at least–and the misogynists.

The woman wasn't young, nor was she particularly old, but she wasn't quite middle-aged either. A late bloomer, with the planet of Neptune conjunct her Midheaven, she had a hard time distinguishing between fantasy and reality.

Astrologically, Neptune rules all things hazy and glamorous, so objectivity and practicality weren't her strong suits. As she strolled through life, she preferred indulging in possibilities and dreams. She often thought of Ferdinand the Bull as her animal totem because taking time to smell the flowers was important to her. And with Neptune in her tenth house—the house of career and vocation—she longed to pursue work that would draw on the images and ideals that flooded her inner world with intensity.

But, it was a challenge, because Saturn marked her ascendant like a toad and a curse.

So the two parts of her personality vied for control over her days (and nights). Whenever the Neptune side broke free from the prison-like constraints Saturn imposed upon her psyche, she was loathe to look back or stop running, because the entire world might turn to salt.

"You can't sing."

It just couldn't be true. Heather Baker slid her Takamine

guitar into its fake-fur-lined case.

Artistic success was 99% perspiration. That meant raw talent accounted for a measly one percent. If you worked hard enough, you could achieve anything. That's what Heather believed, and that's what she would continue to believe.

The woman was just plain wrong—plain and wrong. She'd probably never colored outside the lines.

Heather left the studio and headed for her red Isuzu pickup, every interior entrance and exit in her mind on lockdown. The echoing statement beat against her inner windows and doors like a frenzied bird. She refused to count the number of voice teachers who'd made similar declarations. It was too painful.

Dreams of being on stage and strumming her guitar with a hot flamenco rhythm while she sang like an angel were what kept her going.

She slammed the truck door and gunned the engine.

The problem was chiefly with her diaphragm. It was like a steel plate, jammed high up into her ribcage, unmoving. Nothing like the pliable plastic of a balloon. The diaphragm's muscular flexibility was necessary to provide the uniform release of breath that gave singing notes their tone, control, and color.

No matter how many times Heather lay down with her back pressed against the floor, gulping in quantities of air that made her head spin, her diaphragm resembled boron corbide.

The next problem was her throat. It was clogged, as if she'd swallowed an island when she was four, and it had remained lodged in her windpipe since that unfortunate day.

But she would persevere.

It was her destiny to overcome all obstacles and realize an impossible dream. That was the point of Saturn squaring Neptune in the astrological skies of her natal chart.

At least she had Pluto in her eighth house. The planet of regeneration living in its astrological home would keep her going until she reached a ripe old age. Whether or not she succeeded in any of her endeavors, she would live on and on, to try another day.

It was good news and bad news all around.

When she got home, Heather turned on her computer and began

surfing the net. Maybe she needed a degree, like the scarecrow in the *Wizard of Oz*. Perhaps with the appropriate credentials, her prodigious vocal talents would unleash themselves upon an unsuspecting populace, ala K.T. Oslin. She still had time. Forty wasn't even close. Settling on three musical programs offered within her home state, she drilled down.

The more research she did, the more she realized that a four-year program wasn't going to work. For several reasons, the main three being: finances, finances, and finances. If she was going to make this happen—and she was—she had to face the reality of time constraints.

Damned Saturn! She kicked her bed frame and stubbed her toe. Yelping and dancing around her room, she decided that a two-year program could be perfect.

2. Happy Holidays

Back in those days, before the freeways were like a scene from a bad sci-fi movie, Austin was a healing place. The concentric springs and lakes that surrounded the capitol city of Texas created an energy that set the region apart from the rest of the world. Back then, a spiritual web of eccentrics and new age fanatics, espousing all sorts of implausible philosophies that did little harm to those interested in experimenting with them, existed. Perhaps, it still does.

For Heather, it was like returning year-round to Girl Scout summer camp, which had been one of her most positive formative experiences, especially the singing-around-the-campfire-with-guitars bit.

Ensconced in a cheap apartment and registered in the two-year music program at Austin Community College, she was set.

Music and education. For the moment, Neptune and Saturn were at peace.

The first semester, her favorite class was Guitar Ensemble. Although she was by far the worst guitarist in the class, and was always assigned the most simple, chordal and rhythmic parts, whenever the group performed, her heart swooned. It was as if it had taken wings, discovered an unseen hole in the ceiling, and soared.

Years of painful hours, trapped in cubicles with burlap-like fabric on flimsy walls, and mind-numbing administrative meetings spent deliberating the status of meaningless projects— faded.

Who cared whether or not she could sing? She was alive!

Not that her uncoordinated fingers, and lack of anything but white-people's rhythm didn't offer substantial difficulties, they certainly did, but sometimes, when she strummed her guitar, it actually sounded like music.

Progress on the vocal front proved more challenging as you can imagine.

"There's a voice in there somewhere. We just need find it," her vocal teacher would say. At. Every. Single. Lesson.

Yet no matter what vocal tricks and acrobatics were assigned, drilled, practiced, or attempted, the sweet-spot of Heather's vocal range remained elusive.

She did, however, excel in the study of Music Theory and became adept at sketching music staffs, whole notes, half notes, quarter notes, and eighths—with their little flags, and all the symbols of rest, as well as the curvy symbol for the treble clef.

Late afternoons, spent with her stomach on the floor, darkening the ovals of notes and the rectangles of rests became a meditative oasis. When it came to musical theory, she was something of a natural.

However, when her professor approached her at the end of the semester about changing the focus of her studies from performance to composition, she flinched.

Despite her stellar grades in his class, and her ongoing challenges with singing and playing guitar, the fantasy of becoming the next great indie singer/songwriter still possessed her. The image of herself—transformed into a creature with a mobile diaphragm and nimble fingers—became the siren call, luring her ever onward toward the rocks she was determined to smash herself against.

But she did begin to question herself. At first, it was only a moment here, a nanosecond there.

If she'd stopped to ask the average stranger, Why? Why? Why? her fantastical dreams persisted, they might have said, Because you're an idiot.

But Heather believed in Carl Jung's Theory of Individuation, and she suspected something else was afoot.

Her first epic breakthrough occurred in the holiday season.

"Can you go with me?" Heather asked her friend Bill on the phone. "Moral support."

"Sure. When and where?"

"The old Paramount Theatre on Congress. Tuesday night at 7 p.m."

"Tuesday?"

"I told you, it's not really a performance, it's an audition."

"Right, right, for a Christmas party."

"I can't wait. I'm going to perform *The Little Drummer Boy*.

It's one of my favorite songs ever."

"Pick me up?" Bill asked.

"Around 6:30."

Many of the red velvet seats were moth-eaten. The entire theatre was dingy and pleaded for the attention of enthusiastic house-flippers. Three of the spotlights that rimmed the stage were busted, but Heather—guitar case in hand—felt like she'd arrived at Carnegie Hall.

"Hi!" she introduced herself to Carol Shelton, the woman who'd placed the ad in the *Austin American Statesman* for Christmas talent.

"Are you ready to play?" Carol asked. "No one else is here yet."

Heather searched the Paramount's shadowed recesses. Indeed, she, Carol, and Bill seemed to be the only people in the cavernous hall. Her left toe felt pinched inside her tennis shoe. She'd tied the laces too tight, or maybe the toe of her golf sock was wrinkled. She accepted the twinge of pain along with the dismal turnout.

What the heck. If she got the gig, she'd be playing for an entire party. That thought lifted her spirits right back up. "Sure."

Bill chose a seat out of the hundreds available. Carol sat across the wide central aisle from him. Heather laid her guitar case across several seats in the front row. She lifted out her Takamine, hitched her strap across her neck and shoulder, and advanced to the stage. She positioned herself behind the lonely mic. The working spotlight blinded her. She shaded her eyes with her hand against her brow.

"I'm going to sing *The Little Drummer Boy*," she announced.

She thought she detected a nod from Carol and an encouraging smile from Bill.

Heather shifted her feet, angled the neck of her guitar, and played her best D chord. The first line out of her mouth was mystical—it often was as she sang out full, warm tones from her lower register. Chills chased her spine, and invisible vibrations awakened the empty hall. Unfortunately, her performance didn't ascend with her climb up the vocal ladder. By the third Pa Rum Pum Pum Pum, things scratched, and by the fourth, they squeaked. From there, everything rolled downhill with astonishing speed—each measure gathering strength for the final collision, like the Abominable Snowman turning somersaults down the Alps.

A person more sympathetic to their audience might have cut the song short, but not Heather. Her powerful imagination stepped in, winging her off to some higher plane, where she heard something very different than what Carol and Bill heard.

By the time she'd sung her last note and played her last chord, her heart was ablaze. She interpreted Carol's and Bill's stunned silence as admiration. Under the circumstances, who but she would have persevered?

She'd overcome her nerves—her butterflies had flown in formation.

A more grounded person might have advised her: Honey, those weren't nerves, they were flashing red lights—and you were going in the wrong direction down a one-way street!

But all Heather could think was, My first public audition! And I survived!

Saturn had taught her the value of achieving incremental goals.

"Thank you!" Carol called from afar, as she raced from the building.

Bill's brown eyes were big and round behind his thick bifocals. "I was scared for you."

"Why?" Heather asked.

He jammed his hands deep in his pockets. "Because you were so awful."

"Was I really that bad?"

He nodded.

"But I feel great! It was so fun."

Bill, a writer, a wordsmith, and never speechless, stared at her in dismal silence.

"I mean, I did it," she said.

"Maybe you need more practice," he said.

"I can do that," Heather gushed, for practice was Saturn's domain.

"And maybe you need to sing in a different key."

"How do I figure out which key?" she asked.

Bill's eyes expanded to three times their normal size. "Try the one where you don't go flat on the high notes."

"But how did I look?" she asked. "What do you think of my hair?"

After going red earlier in the summer, it had taken three trips to the salon to turn her naturally brunette hair platinum.

Bill yanked on a strand. "You looked awesome."

"Thanks."

He picked up her guitar case. "Have you ever considered acting?" he asked as they exited the theater.

"Yes, but I didn't like it."

"Why not?" he asked. "I bet you'd be good at it."

"I find it creepy," she admitted. "When I took a class, I realized I've been acting my entire life. So when I get on stage, and try to pretend to be someone else, it's really disorienting. The truth is: These days I'm trying to find myself, not be someone else. Plus, speaking words that someone else wrote makes me feel like a cypher."

Bill opened the door of her truck for her. "I see what you mean."

Heather settled in her seat. "It's disappointing that Carol left without giving me any feedback on my audition. I would have loved to know what she thought."

"Yeah." He slammed the door abruptly.

Later that night, at home and alone in her apartment, Heather reflected on the awesome experience. It didn't matter that every note hadn't been perfect. The rush of being on stage, of doing something she'd never believed she could possibly do, but had always desperately wanted to try, drowned out Bill's pointed critique of her performance and the fact that Carol hadn't hired her for the party.

A teeny smile crept upon her lips. She let it stay.

3. The Cherry Lane Coffee Co.

In her second semester of the music program, Heather enrolled in a midi class. Computers and music. She had some background in computers and was curious. There was a fellow student in her class who was even older than she was. She liked him because he asked all the dumb questions she would have asked if he hadn't been there.

Their young teacher didn't care for either of them.

Heather didn't mind. She'd become fascinated with programming musical arrangements and could see she had a lot to learn.

That same semester, she also took a class in Audio Production. It was high time she set up a home recording studio. With the help of her AP teacher, she put together an inventory of equipment to build the most basic studio. A Sennheiser mic,

Monster coax cables, a Mackie 12-channel mixer, a Yamaha 4-track Cassette Recorder, two Alesis monitors, a low-end Korg synth, and some bulk speaker wire. She drove the eighty miles to Hermes Music Store in San Antonio, Texas to pick everything up. It had the best prices on gear.

Back in her apartment, she unpacked her toys. When she grinned, her gaze flitted to the window—to be sure no one saw her.

Now, it was time for the real work to begin. Time to produce that first CD.

Heather pulled out a manila folder, crammed with loose sheets of paper in varying sizes and color. The disarray amounted to lyrics for about forty songs, written over the years in uneven bursts of inspiration. She sifted through them and sorted them along the lines of her favorites. After she narrowed them down to twenty, she grabbed the stack, stuffed them into her purse, and headed to the Cherry Lane Coffee Co.

A couple of espresso shots should help her zero in on the twelve gems to record first.

The coffee shop was quiet at four o'clock in the afternoon. One of the regular baristas made Heather's Americano with steamed heavy whipping cream. Her favorite overstuffed chair was available. She blanketed the long, low table in front of the chair with her heart and soul.

The more she studied the words she'd written, the more she spotted the nuggets of unflinching truth they revealed.

The question was: How honest did she want to be for the sake of art?

Appearing on *The Dr. Phil Show* seemed awfully low brow. Could creating a CD of confessional songs be considered the equivalent?

With knees tucked beneath her, she sipped her coffee.

"What's got you so happy?" The barista swept the stone floor a few feet away. "Love letters or something?"

Heather jumped, a slosh of lukewarm coffee spilled onto her wrist. "No, no, not love letters."

The young woman swept closer to where Heather sat. "What then? I've never seen you smile like that."

Had she been—smiling?

"Uhm, you know, they're just, uhm, some things I wrote a

while back," Heather squeaked. Her brain had split in two. By any objective standards, the lyrics she'd written were by turns bleak and pretentious, haunting and overwrought, poetic and far too literal. Why had she been smiling?

"I figured you for a writer or something."

"You did?"

"Yeah. Always alone and scribbling," the young woman said.

What was she supposed to say to that? "Oh."

"I'll let you get back to it," the young woman drifted off.

A strange feeling seeped into Heather's heart. It was like, for a single moment, she was exactly where she was supposed to be, doing exactly what she was supposed to be doing.

Maybe it was just the caffeine.

She went back to studying her songs. She had to admit there was something invigorating about the dark, angsty lyrics. A few of them, two or three, were even hopeful.

Shuffling the papers around, a theme emerged.

The truth will set you free.

Did she dare tell it? After all these years, was there even a point?

She pressed her lips together, then puckered them into a trout pout, before wiggling them back and forth.

Heather believed in catharsis.

She ordered another Americano. By the time she left, she'd selected twelve songs and arranged them in the proper sequence to take the listener on a journey through the dark night of the soul and back out into the light.

All the way to her apartment, she hummed the tune to *You Didn't Win*.

If she was smiling, no one would have seen.

The sun had already set.

4. A Strange Turn

Producing a music CD entailed more work than Heather had imagined.

By the time she graduated from her two-year music program, she was still banging away in the anvil of her music studio, like a clone of the logo on the Sound Forge music software she'd recently purchased.

Unfortunately, her Neptunian idyll had drawn to an end. Saturn reared its cranky head and demanded the bills be paid. Time to get a job.

And even though she still couldn't sing that well, and her guitar playing was better suited to a marching band that strictly adhered to 4/4 beats, she'd been told she was writing interesting chord progressions, and most people were impressed with her lyrics.

All in all, it was heartening. And she was more determined than ever to finish her first CD.

And this is where the story takes a strange turn. It was as if Heather had a fairy godmother who watched over her from the heavens. It took only a slip of her foot and a twist of an ankle for Heather to wake up one morning, standing in front of the tall building on Holcombe Boulevard in Houston, Texas.

Delivered, as if by an enchanted pumpkin morphed into a carriage, she couldn't quite grasp how she'd arrived at this, the first day of her new job. Common sense demanded that her two-year work hiatus would have meant poor prospects and a significant pay cut. Certainly, potential employers would have scanned the gaps in her resume and written words like: *unreliable* and *flighty* with thick red markers across her application.

Yet, that wasn't what had happened at all. It was as if—by magic —her commitment to her dreams and ideals had unlocked, heretofore, hidden qualities in her nature. Odd abilities to communicate and connect with other people had surfaced, attributes she'd never consciously sought to cultivate. More importantly, after two years of facing her worst fears and surviving, she'd become more truly herself.

That was something she couldn't see when she looked in the mirror, but others sensed it. They seemed more than ever to like having her around. Facing her own limitations, and coming up against the immutable wall of her diaphragm, had somehow softened the rest of her insides—knocking all vestiges of judgment from her, like a tough wind. And even when she said nothing, people knew she understood: life is difficult.

So it seemed that being *real*, more than being magnificent and in possession of some earth-shattering talent, had mined a few of Saturn's treasures—one being the highest paying job in her life.

It was an unexpected turn of events.

Though she didn't know it that morning, Neptune was going to deliver pretty soon, too.

The first few months on her new job, Heather often worked late. When most of her coworkers were gone, she'd dig into the pile of projects that towered on her desk. One night, the janitor whistled as he emptied her trashcan. Distracted by the tune, she took a good look at him.

They struck up a conversation that quickly turned to music. He played bass in a band. Not a gig-playing band, but a band that also had a guitar player, a keyboard player, and a drummer. One thing led to another, and they agreed to meet one afternoon. She would bring a few of her songs.

A few weeks later, in a garage across town, he introduced her to his bandmates. With little small talk, they took the xeroxed tablatures she gave them for her song *New World*. The chord structure was simple, and she liked the riff that she'd written for the guitar. The guys took the sheets and began noodling. Within a few minutes, the sounds melded.

She basked in the amazing experience of their interpretation. The impact of a group of musicians, bringing her song to life, stunned her. Never before having considered working with a band, she changed her mind on the spot.

For the next several months, she posted classified ads—even considering other singers for lead vocals. It was a whirlwind of experience and colorful personalities, but by Thanksgiving, she had to face the fact that the collaborative element of scheduling and working with a group was beyond her.

But once again, the experience had unleashed a new level of confidence.

Some of the best guitar players at the open mics she'd been too had wanted to talk with her about the chord changes she'd written, and other elements of her composition. It wasn't like being discovered, but it was like being part of a tribe.

And sometimes, in spite of herself, she smiled at her day job.

It seemed that someone else took notice:

A man—who invited her to lunch. He asked her to marry him.

Which she did.

The whirlwind romance scandalized their coworkers—scandal being Neptune's domain.

He'd been a confirmed bachelor and claimed she'd put a spell on him. Heather thought the real scandal was how Neptune had dissolved her mask of frowns and grimaces, which had kept her heart guarded for decade, upon the delivery of her soul mate.

Because when she was with him, she couldn't help but smile.

It was a puzzling turn of events and made her doubt herself in a brand new way (doubt being Saturn's wheelhouse). Sometimes, when she was struggling with one of the tracks of her old songs, she would wonder, was I ever really that sad?

When she contemplated the album artwork, which she'd sketched before she'd met her soul mate, she'd wonder, did I ever really feel that damaged?

The questions would keep her up at night, wandering their love-filled home in despair. Contentment was a stranger, a form of affront. Had happiness made a liar of her?

The inner gap widened when she saw the Grand Canyon. They had driven by it, when her husband whisked her off to California —because living in that most western state had been high on both their bucket lists, even before they'd met.

When they made their new home in San Diego, it didn't go unnoticed by either that they now lived within driving distance of Los Angeles—that great mecca where all dreams come true.

Although sometimes, in unexpected ways.

5. Messengers and Moments

The cross-country move and her new role as wife left Heather feeling disoriented and unfamiliar to herself.

She began to meditate upon *The Ugly Duckling* for she'd often imagined herself as a misplaced swan. But with all the changes, and her sadness shedding like the skin of a snake, she'd stare in the mirror and whisper, "Perhaps, you're not even a bird."

Finding a new animal totem became imperative. She searched the traits of other creatures online for hours. She was torn between turtles and tigers. Turtles were ancient and endangered. They had hard shells like shields. Although carnivores when young, they could survive on plants, if pressed. Recently, Heather had begun to experiment with veganism, but according to her Chinese horoscope, she was a tiger.

In the mornings, after her husband left for work, she would

growl and roar at herself in the mirror. By lunchtime, she'd feel uncertain.

As she drifted through this strange new passage in life, her feet barely touched the ground. Perhaps, living in proximity to the ocean had given Neptune the upper hand.

"Or did I just leave Saturn in Texas?" she wondered, missing her melancholy.

Because as much as she resented the painstaking lessons that Saturn had foisted upon her from the moment of birth, all-in-all she'd come to realize the planet possessed a certain charm. Wisdom, patience, and sturdy foundations were nothing to sneeze at.

"Ready?" George Nash, the owner of The Metaphor Cafe, asked.

"Yes," Heather said.

"All right." When he crossed his arms, the purple cover of her CD, *The Faith of a Crucified Child*, disappeared from sight—whether it was clamped to his side, or behind his back, she couldn't tell. Not that the specifics mattered.

But she liked seeing the fruits of her labor. The talisman

fortified her. It reminded her that she'd produced a CD that told a story. It was a sad story, perhaps to some, a troubling or unsettling one, but Heather didn't see it that way anymore. To her, the story of a child's experience of their parents' divorce, and the predictable blended family that followed, had become a common one.

Yet, often, after hearing the CD, friends and acquaintances would have a puzzled look in their eyes. Were they trying to reconcile the zany, laughing, late-blooming woman she'd become, with the tortured, Mary-Daly-Andrea-Dworkin-reading rabid feminist who'd penned her first oeuvre? Or were they just shocked by the fact that she was slowly beginning to accept: No matter how hard she tried, she really couldn't sing?

Hard to say.

Stepping away from the stage, George nodded, smiling, encouraging, hopeful.

Heather took a deep breath and began to sing.

Within two minutes, every single customer in the cafe had relocated from the inside tables to the ones lining the sidewalk. It was a balmy afternoon in Escondido, CA, and they just wanted to enjoy the fresh air. All of them. At the exact moment she'd begun to sing.

George stared at the floor, shoulders dropped.

Heather soldiered on.

When she was done, George looked up. "Did you relax your throat like I told you?"

How to explain it was a physiological impossibility?

Although she hadn't given up completely, day after day her enthusiasm waned.

Fortunately, her quest for gigs had led her to George, who believed in her as much as her husband did. In moments like this, her new mission in life had become to not let either of them down.

George waved her to a table in the corner.

With great relief, Heather left the stage and joined him.

He tapped her CD on the table. "You're a messenger."

The definitive way he said the words made them sound prophetic. Heather gulped. She tilted her head and searched his craggy face. "Messenger of what?" she asked.

"The truth," he said. "A truth."

Something stirred in her chest, maybe an inkling of comprehension. She absorbed the moment. Despite the fact that she still couldn't sing, receiving George's message, and sitting at this table in the Metaphor Cafe, in Escondido, CA, was something of a miracle. Her mind traveled backwards.

If she'd never tried to sing, she wouldn't be here.

There was no logic to the story, only a reality that seemed spun by magic. This was a transcendent moment. One she would always treasure.

She was a messenger.

6. My Name is Heather Baker, Welcome to My World

A year later, the Metaphor Cafe closed. However Neptune, in the guise of music, had two more lessons to teach Heather.

Over the past year, she'd befriended more musicians on the local scene and become enamored with live music. Perhaps, part of her performance problems were the mechanized rhythms of her music tracks. What would it be like to pause and breathe, to follow the beat of her very human heart?

Almost like Pinocchio becoming a real boy.

She'd ditched her guitar when she'd discovered midi, but now she wanted to give the keyboard a shot. Today, she sat on a piano bench next to Jimmy Longo. Jimmy was a true musician. He played in a gig-playing band, taught students, and booked talent for the world-famous Twigg's Green Room—a venue Heather longed to play at.

He had her juggling tennis balls, listening to The Gypsies, and learning to play off-beat. It was slow going, but she sensed something transforming in her brain. Perhaps, her right and left hemispheres were finally communicating.

Jimmy often told her, "Don't stop before the magic happens."

She began to wonder if he just needed the money she paid for her lessons, because as with her vocal lessons at Austin Community College, noticeable improvement eluded her.

Then one day, he brought his violin to her lesson.

She'd been composing varying rhythmic riffs to the chord changes of the Beatles song, *Let it Be*, as he'd instructed. After she warmed up, he took his violin out of the case and indicated for her to keep playing. When he joined her, a golden light danced in the air between them.

He smiled and nodded.

Jimmy, the gods, and the faeries were her only witness when inner lightning struck. Something about who she was shifted forever. She grasped the powerful nature of the ephemeral—the perfect, unrepeatable moment. After working hard for twelve years, she'd arrived at a new threshold and crossed over it in the blink of an eye.

That was the nature of life and magic.

A new zest consumed her. They'd begun videotaping her shows, so she could study them with the hopes of improving. Along the way, she got an idea to make a DVD. The story around her songs.

The product, *My Name is Heather Baker, Welcome to My World*, got a two-thumbs up from her old mentor George. She booked more shows at Borders, the Hot Java Cafe, Lestat's, and finally, she got a date at Twigg's Green Room.

That night was something of a disaster. In many ways, it was similar to her first audition, years ago. More and more, she felt out of sync with her old material. She'd changed so much that she needed new songs. Cruising the music section on Amazon one day for inspiration, she came across the book, *The Frustrated Songwriter's Handbook*. Something about the idea of immersion composition intrigued her.

In her prior life, Heather followed the rules and read books cover to cover.

Not anymore. When the handbook arrived, she rifled through it. The chapter on *The Day Session* caught her eye—a scheduled twelve-hour block to write a lot of music. Not good music—just a lot of music. The goal: mental exhaustion. Apparently, the book's authors believed a tapped-out brain was capable of producing some of the most interesting musical and lyrical ideas.

Heather had been exposed to stranger notions. The day she gave it a go she produced the five best songs she'd ever written. It was unnerving the way the experience upended her beliefs about productivity. Apparently, a bottomless pit of creativity lurked within and mental exhaustion was one of the best buckets to retrieve the gold.

She couldn't decide if that was good news or bad news.

Unaware that she had just learned the final lesson her musical journey would impart, Heather booked a few more shows at Borders. Before the last one, she got the call. Her grandmother was coming home from the hospital, not to recoup, but to enter hospice.

She made her flight reservations and canceled that last show.

She sat next to the hospital bed that the medical supply people had delivered a week earlier. Propped up, her grandmother wore a knit wool hat. The burnt reds and oranges clashed with her pale pink and blue pajamas. She was having one of her spells. One moment burning alive, the next freezing cold.

"Children, my children, what are you doing to me?" her grandmother moaned. "I'm so hot."

Heather pulled the cap off her grandmother's head and fussed with the messy gray wisps it left behind.

Her grandmother stretched out her hand, blindly patting the silver rail of her bed. "Is that you, Heather?"

"Yes, Grandma. We're trying to make you feel better, but I guess we're not doing a very good job."

Her grandmother squeezed Heather's hand, kicked her leg high in the air like a child, and laughed. She peered through the bed's railings. "Is that right?"

"Yes," Heather whispered.

Her grandmother patted her hand. "Well, that's all right."

That laugh, that gaze, that gesture, that brief moment of joy, were the last lucid moments of her grandmother's life.

When the sacred moment of death came, the new loss carved another hole and space in Heather's heart. With no children of her own, to whom would she give all that her grandmother had given her?

Again, she spent her days wandering her house.

At long last, she faced her Yamaha digital piano and admitted that she was too tired and had become too old to cart the thing around town.

It was a whimpering, yet definitive, end of an era.

What surprised her was the ecstatic sense of relief that washed over her. She'd expected the doom of her failed dreams and ambition to crush her, but letting go of her unrealized hopes buoyed her. A new peace settled in heart. Such a mystery was this quiet space to breathe and look around with no agenda.

She began to meditate upon *Goldilocks and the Three Bears*. Her day job hadn't engaged enough of her imagination, the bowl of porridge too cold. Her vision of herself as a breakout indie singer/songwriter had engaged more imagination than was possible for her to manifest in this lifetime—the bowl of porridge too hot.

Surely, out there somewhere was the bowl of porridge just right.

However, no longer desperate, and having lived in the arms of love for the better part of a decade, Heather trusted that the right bowl would appear of its own volition.

It took an entire year, but one day she found herself researching fairy tales at the public library. Perhaps, one day, she would dare to write one of her own.

One morning, months later, she turned on her computer and began to type. As the words flowed, she became aware of how well her musical journey had prepared her for this particular moment. With Neptune's inspiration peeking over one shoulder, and Saturn's discipline settled upon the other, writing fairy tales felt…just right.

Several years later, Heather was watching the TV show *American Idol* with her husband.

"What was that?" she asked, when one of her favorite contestants hadn't performed at his peak.

"He was flat," her husband said.

"Really? I couldn't tell."

She and her husband looked at one another, eyebrows raised.

"Tell me when it happens again," she said.

By the end of the night, it had become clear, she was partially tone deaf. The realization made her laugh so hard she almost fell off the couch.

All along, she'd thought it was her diaphragm.

Thank You

I appreciate you spending your valuable time reading *The Girl who Believed in Fairy Tales*. If you'd like to share the story with other readers, please tell a friend, or post a review on any book-ish site.

I'd also like to invite you to sign up for my newsletter: http://eepurl.com/wWKUj. It's quirky—like me:D—and I confess, it comes out sporadically, but I send a variety of things, including some (hopefully) pleasant surprises along with updates on all my new releases.

Sincerely,

Acknowledgment

Jason Gurley generously contributed design concepts and supervision for the development of the cover.

First Chapter of Dreaming of the Sea Paperback

2005 –

Nine-year-old Miriam clutched her pink sock monkey as she stared at the television. Perched on the edge of the sofa, because she could never properly balance in the enormous and uncomfortable dip in its middle, she ran her tongue over the ridges of her chapped lower lip. When she found a bit of loose skin she chewed it off. It was impossible to concentrate on what Ernie and the Cookie Monster were saying. The escalating grunts and murmurs coming from the apartment's single bedroom split her attention, even though the door was closed.

It was winter, and the apartment was cold. As the sun set, the temperature inside became frigid. Miriam's oversized sweats and thin t-shirt offered little warmth as the living room darkened. Her mother often turned off the heat to save money. Miriam rubbed her eyes. The two hours of Sesame Street reruns were almost finished. Her favorite show, My Little Pony, was next. Her stomach gurgled. She glanced at the closed bedroom door and strained her ears. They must be passed out. If she was lucky they'd remain that way until morning, and Miriam would be at school when the bedroom door finally opened.

Sometimes she got lucky.

The kitchen and living room were one space, separated by a counter. On the way to the pantry, Miriam carefully stepped around the squeaky spot beneath the stained carpet. Besides the ends of a loaf of bread in a knotted plastic sack, there wasn't much on the shelves. Jars of peanut butter, mustard, pickle relish, and a few cans of Campbell soup. A bowl of soup would warm her up, but she couldn't risk banging the pot against the stove. A peanut butter and jelly sandwich would have to do.

Miriam reached for the bread and peanut butter. She set them down softly on the kitchen counter. She stood before the refrigerator and sucked in her breath. If she wasn't careful, the door would make a loud smack when it closed. Maybe she should forget the jelly.

She glanced back at the bedroom door. It remained safely closed. A peanut butter and jelly sandwich would taste so good. Miriam yanked on the refrigerator door. Light spilled out. It was as empty as the pantry, but there was a half-full jar of grape jelly on the side door. She eased it out. With her other hand, she gripped the door handle. When it was almost closed, she let go. It made a slight pop as it sealed. Miriam froze.

Her pulse pounded in her ears as she slowly turned. Miriam screamed and dropped the jar. It rolled across the floor until it banged against the bottom of the refrigerator.

The man her mother had brought home earlier leaned with his elbows against the counter, watching her. His long stringy hair reached past his shoulders. Miriam couldn't begin to count the number of tattoos on the threatening bare skin of his arms and chest.

She backed away as he came around the counter and picked up the jelly.

He pulled open the refrigerator and slid the jar next to a six-pack of beer. He crouched down in front of Miriam, who stood with her back against the wall. "You can have dinner after we play."

Miriam's stomach heaved. He took her hand. She refused to walk. He pulled harder. Her sock-covered feet slid.

"She doesn't want to come," he shouted to Miriam's mother.

Lights flicked on in the bedroom.

Once attractive, Helen now looked used up. Gaunt and sallow, a belt circled her bicep. She staggered toward the man and her daughter. "Hey, honey, don't you want to play fashion model?"

Miriam's eyes welled with tears. Fashion models wore clothes.

The 1500s –

Once upon a time, a woman tempted to throw herself from a seaside cliff onto the killing rocks below paused to reconsider: Would it be more satisfying if her lover could feel the agony that ripped her heart to shreds and pulverized its remaining tissue with meaty blows? Yes, she thought. Revenge would be more sweet than immolation.

Her plea, so genuine and determined, reached the devil's ear. It was just the kind of dilemma he relished.

When he arrived on the blustery promontory, he paid his

compliments. "In the throes of devastating betrayal, few have the presence of mind to stop and think. Yet how much more satisfying than suicide is an eye for an eye—a tooth for a tooth—a heart for a heart."

The woman seethed. She dug her fingernails into her palms, drawing blood. The devil caught a whiff. He encouraged her to confide her tale.

"The man I believed mine—" The woman banged her wounded hand against her breast. Two drops of blood speckled the front of her simple dress. She broke down, hiccoughing, before she wiped her tears away, leaving a smear of blood from her cheek to her chin. "He's a sailor. His easy lies concealed wives, lovers, and children. He abandons them in every port like stray dogs. I found proof in a wooden chest he keeps locked away in his boat. Oh, he denied it all, until I shoved those love letters and trinkets down his throat." She laughed, it was a gash to the ears. "After he choked them up, he gloated over my naiveté. 'Did you think you were the only one?'" The woman moaned.

"I know of a volcano," the devil said, for he'd contrived an elegant solution.

The woman listened with every pore.

"It's at the bottom of the sea and needs tending."

"What kind of care does a volcano require, especially one on the ocean floor?"

"It would be better if it had some kind of guardian," the devil's tone was matter-of-fact; it always was when ploughing the ground for the purchase of a soul. "A witch is what I'm thinking," he said.

"What kind of a witch?"

"A sea witch."

"And how will that suit my need for revenge?"

"Oh, it will suit your need very well. I'll grant you the ability to draw from the volcano's raw power. In its proximity, you'll control the very sea. And it's not far from here." The devil pointed to the cove. "Your man, does he sail these waters with some frequency?" He drew a square in the air between the visible shore and the sea's horizon.

"Yes, his routes are most commonly in these waters."

"Then you might conjure a sea storm, and when his wrecked ship sinks to the ocean floor, you could salvage his bones. Make some little knickknacks with them."

"Where would I keep them?"

The devil stroked his goatee, for he'd chosen an urbane facade. "You would need a lair, I think. A place of your own, in the volcano's shadow."

"But I can't live underwater!"

"Ah." The devil clasped his hands behind his back. The movement pulled open his grey tweed jacket and exposed his fine white shirt, satin vest, and the gold chain of a pocket watch. He liked to attend to details when he made these appearances. "I've forgotten to mention the best part haven't I?" The woman's puzzled expression encouraged him. She would agree to the pact, he was certain. "There are creatures who inhabit the sea— light-filled vermin who sing and celebrate all the time. They're rather annoying in their banality." He sniffed. "Perhaps you've heard of them. They're called mermaids."

"Oh, they're nothing but storybook creatures—they're not real."

"I assure you they are." The devil put his hands in his pockets and made a half-turn. "Walk with me."

She followed along beside him.

"Let's say, you're not only the volcano's custodian, but you're also given the power to take and restore the ability to live in the sea." He paused his stride. "You could take a mermaid's fins and replace them with legs. Or you could take a mortal's legs and replace them with fins." He released his chin and waved a hand in the air. "Of course, you'd have the talent for the usual spells and draughts too. "

The woman held up her hand and ticked off the devil's promises. "Keeper of the volcano, ability to create sea storms, giver and taker of fins and legs, talent for spells and draughts, plus my own little cottage on the ocean floor."

"Yes, yes, of course."

It all sounded to good to be true. "You'll be wanting something from me, I suppose."

"Only your soul."

The woman wasn't the god-fearing type; she wasn't even convinced she had a soul. "That's all, my soul?"

"With the many powers I'm bestowing upon you, and given the blackness roiling in your heart, I imagine you'll be up to all sorts of no good. You don't want to have to pay for all that in the afterlife, do you?"

The woman snorted. "Of course not."

"Didn't think so. The day you die, I'll harvest your soul and leave you to slumber peacefully through eternity."

The woman liked to sleep. "And if you don't take my soul? What will happen to me then?"

"That will depend on the the quality of your choices while you're alive."

"Then it's true, all that stuff about heaven and hell," the woman murmured. Being no saint, she hated to think of the crimes she might already be spiritually indebted for.

"Very true."

"Maybe it's better if I don't–"

"Have to take responsibility for any of your actions."

"Exactly." She considered his proposition a bit more and realized she'd come out on top. "I don't know why more folks don't deal directly with you."

"It's a mystery to me as well." The devil chuckled. "There is one more small matter."

The woman's fantasies of extracting vengeance from her lover came to a halt. What more could there be?

"It would be splendid if you could locate an apprentice who'll take your place before you die," the devil said. "In fact, I think I'll make that part of the contract."

The woman plucked at her dress. "But how will I find one?"

The devil gave her question some thought. "I see your point. It would be hard, if not impossible, to convince one of those simpering mermaids to take your place. Perhaps you should be amphibious," he mused.

"What does that mean?"

"You'll be able to walk on land and swim in the sea. You'll be the only one who can."

"You mean I'll have legs when I'm not in the water?"

"Yes, and fins when you're in the sea. Rather ingenious, don't you think? It will make it much easier to find a mortal to serve as your apprentice."

"Oh, all right. I suppose that's not too much to ask."

"I thought not."

And so, the first sea witch in a long line of sea witches came into being.

1852 –

Nine-year-old Gertrude lazed on a pile of rubble outside the sea witch's lair. The stack of rotting clothes, disintegrating maps, and swathes of decomposing canvas, which had once waved in sea breezes and snapped in crosswinds as proud sails, overflowed a warped crate re-shaped to Gertrude's body. The make-shift couch was the sea witch's apprentice preferred spot to kill time.

In the depths of her lair, Beulah, gulped and sputtered. The sea witch was a noisy sleeper. At least she wasn't nagging Gertrude to collect fecal pellets, fungi, sea urchin spines, or worms this afternoon. Gertrude chewed on a thumbnail. No matter how assiduously she gnawed the thick, gray thing, it never broke or splintered. In her peripheral vision, the snake-like coils of her hair writhed as if they were alive. She did her best to ignore them as she passed some gas. As usual, she'd eaten too much mush.

Beulah boiled water spiders, water snakes, and water bugs over kettles of lava extracted from the nearby volcano. The tasty stew was the only thing about being the sea witch's apprentice that Gertrude liked, and she always ate too much of it.

She shifted on the mound of trash as another puff of wind escaped her blob-shaped body. Her gaze followed the yellow-green cloud until it collided with a glimmer of light. What's this? Gertrude pushed herself up onto her wrists.

The glow swam in her direction. It haloed a creature unlike any Gertrude had ever seen. Her eyes widened at the sight of the silky golden hair, creamy complexion, and graceful tail fin covered in a mosaic of shimmering scales.

"Are you the sea witch?" the creature trilled.

Gertrude gaped and shook her head.

"Do you know where she lives?"

Gertrude pointed to the dark opening behind her. "What are you?" she asked the creature in her rough voice.

"A mermaid."

"I'll tell Beulah you're here."

"Thank you." The mermaid twirled her slim hands in graceful spirals, treading water.

"Beulah!" Gertrude yelled. Her eyes remained on the mermaid's pearly fingernails.

"What are you yapping about now?" Beulah grumbled from the lair's interior.

"Are you here for a spell?" Gertrude tried to soften her voice, but it came out more like a hiss.

The mermaid arched backward as she nodded.

"Customer!" Gertrude yelled. "Go on inside."

The mermaid hesitated before swishing her sparkly tail to propel her into the depths of the sea witch's lair.

Inside, Beulah sat on her own throne of trash. "Well, what do you want?"

"I need legs—human ones. I've been told you have the power to—" The mermaid's graceful tail went limp under the gaze of Beulah's beady eyes. "Grant my wish."

"I don't grant anything." Beulah ran her finger over a pile of bottles filled with rays of fluorescent gold, blue, green, and pink. "My potions and spells are costly."

Gertrude thought the mermaid's eyes watered. Although, at the bottom of the sea, it was always hard to tell.

"I don't have any gold."

"No? That's too bad."

"I must have a pair of human legs." The mermaid's hands fluttered to her chest. "I've fallen in love."

"Of course you have," Beulah snickered. "Do you have anything of value?"

The mermaid blinked her blue eyes. "Why, I don't know."

Beulah grunted. "If you can't pay for the potion, you won't be getting any legs."

Gertrude watched the exchange with increasing interest. "Do you have any jewelry?"

The mermaid gave her head a sorrowful shake.

"Maybe you know where a treasure chest is buried?" Gertrude prompted, although she wasn't exactly sure why she wanted to help the mermaid.

"No," the mermaid whispered.

"Then go on. Get of here." Beulah waved her lumpy arms.

"I can sing," the mermaid said. "I've been told I have a beautiful voice."

Beulah's brow creased. "Let me hear a song."

The mermaid closed her eyes and clasped her hands. Even though her sweet-sounding voice quavered and trembled, it was a delicate and alluring sound.

When she was finished singing, Beulah's eyes narrowed. "I'll trade your voice for a pair of legs."

The mermaid agreed.

"You understand you won't ever be able to speak again, and every time you take a step on those human legs it's going to feel like you're walking on a pair of knives."

Gertrude thought the mermaid's eyes were tearing up again,

even as she clung to the bargain.

"All trades are final. There's no taking it back if your human doesn't return your love."

The mermaid fluttered her eyelashes. "I understand."

"Well, then."

Gertrude hovered nearby as the sea witch boiled some worms and crab eyes.

Beulah tossed two handfuls of smashed snail shells into the pot as she muttered an incantation. At the last minute the sea witch whipped out her free hand to catch a handful of her apprentice's skirt. "Bring me the yellow one and the blue one." The sea witch pointed to the coral-colored vials on the shelf of bones.

Gertrude obeyed.

Beulah stirred all of the yellow elixir and half of the blue into the pot before refilling each vial with the bubbling ingredients. Now, the liquid in the first vial was a muddy brown and the liquid in the second was a deep, slimy green. Beulah gave the muddy brown potion to the mermaid. "It will scrape your throat going down, but when it comes back up it will bring your voice with it."

The mermaid's pale skin turned paler.

"Get the bucket," Beulah ordered Gertrude. When her

apprentice had the rusted pail in hand, the sea witch told the mermaid to drink up.

She did.

"Every last drop," Beulah croaked.

The drained vial slipped from the mermaid's fingers. Her lips pursed, her eyes rolled, she clutched her throat, her entire body convulsed.

Gertrude couldn't believe anyone would willingly undergo such treatment for anything.

When the mermaid began to choke, Beulah shoved the swamp green vial at Gertrude at the same time she grabbed the bucket from her. "Don't just stand there like an idiot. You have to catch her voice!"

A radiant spittle erupted from the mermaid's small mouth.

Beulah captured every drop. Her black eyes shined with glee.

When the mermaid opened her mouth, she winced. No sound came out.

"Your throat is raw. It will heal in time. But you'll never speak or sing again." Beulah cackled.

For the first time Gertrude truly contemplated the power that would someday be hers.

Beulah told her apprentice to give the mermaid the second potion. "Don't take it until you're on land. Otherwise you might drown." The sea witch cackled again. "It's going to feel like someone is sawing off your tail fin and nailing legs in its place. But maybe your human will return your love, and it will all be worth it."

The mermaid's eyes remained downcast as she draped the vial's chain around her neck then hurriedly exited the lair.

Gertrude was full of questions. "Why are we so ugly?"

"Witches must be fierce creatures." The sea witch nodded toward the retreating mermaid. "Who would be afraid of her?"

"Maybe fear isn't the only kind of power. Did you see how even the eels stopped to look at her?"

Beulah whacked Gertrude on the side of the head. "Be grateful for what you've got." The sea witch smashed a handful of poached sea beetles into her mouth. "There's lots of girls who'd be glad to take your place. Your mother did you a favor by bringing you to me early on. You've got lots of time to study and develop your cunning. By the time I'm gone, you'll be one of the most powerful sea witches who ever lived."

Gertrude never liked to be reminded of her mother who'd

traded her to the sea witch for a love potion when Gertrude was still an infant. "It would be easier to understand why the mermaid wanted to trade her tail fin if she had a black snake tail like you and me."

Beulah cuffed her again. "Nothing is wrong with our tails, girl."

The back of Gertrude's head smarted.

"If you ask me, that mermaid is stupid," Beulah squawked.

"What are you going to do with her voice?"

"Hoard it." Beulah gave Gertrude's ear a painful tweak. "I don't like to let go of anything. You never know when it might come in handy."

"Have you ever been on land?" Gertrude asked her mentor.

"Last time I went up there, I got you. I don't want for anything else. Taking trips is a waste of time if you ask me. Home sweet home is my motto."

Gertrude fell silent. Beulah, often exhausted after working magic, spread out on a trough of bones.

When the sea witch began to snore, her apprentice swam after the mermaid. Hiding in the shadows, Gertrude tried to catch up with the mesmerizing creature.

By the time Gertrude reached the border of their waters, the mermaid's light had receded to a faint flicker overhead.

Gertrude watched the slim ray of light as it continued to ascend. After it disappeared, she began to wonder: If her hair was smooth and flowing, not snake-like; if her complexion was fair, not pocked and scarred; if her form was comely, not in the shape of a blob with crooked hands and teeth protruding, would she be more powerful than Beulah?

It set Gertrude to dreaming.

About the Author

Heidi Garrett is the author of the *Daughter of Light* fantasy trilogy about a young half-faerie, half-mortal searching for her place in the Whole.

She's also the author of *Once Upon a Time Today*, a collection of modern fairy tale retellings for adults who have already left home. *The Magic Cupcake* series is paranormal romance trilogy she writes with Billie Limpin.

Heidi was born in Texas, and attempted to reside in as many cities in that state as possible. She made it to Houston, Lubbock, Austin, and El Paso. After spending a decade in southern California, she now lives in Eastern Washington state with her husband, their two cats, her laptop, and her Kindle. Being from the South, she often contemplates the magic of snow.

You can find Heidi on her blog.

www.ingramcontent.com/pod-product-compliance
Lightning Source LLC
Chambersburg PA
CBHW060426130626
46555CB00003D/2236

9780988206885